DARE TO HOLD

Meg Thompson & Scott Dare
Dare to Love Series #6

NEW YORK TIMES BESTSELLING AUTHOR
Carly Phillips

NY Times Bestselling Author Carly Phillips turns up the heat in her newest sexy contemporary romance series, and introduces you to the Dare family… siblings shaped by a father's secrets and betrayal.

Some women always get it right. Kindergarten teacher, Meg Thompson, on the other hand, consistently makes the wrong decisions—and she is currently single, pregnant and alone. Meg is determined to make changes in her life, to be a better mother than her own had been. No revolving door of men. No man, period. Just a single-minded focus on her baby. Her resolution would be easier to keep if not for hot cop, Scott Dare. He insinuates himself in her life, making Meg want to believe in happily ever after, even if history has taught her to know better.

When Scott Dare hears Meg's friends are determined she have a night of hot sex, before her life changes forever, he decides that man must be him. Their one night is mind blowing and life altering. And Scott, a man already burned by his ex-wife, finds himself all in anyway. While protecting Meg from her violent ex and becoming part of her increasingly complicated life, he's falling hard and he can't seem to find distance. Not when their bodies respond to each other with such heated intensity and he's drawn to her unique combination of strength and vulnerability.

But Meg's future is one Scott has accepted he'll never have, even if his growing feelings say otherwise …

"Carly Phillips is synonymous with red-hot romance and passionate love."
—Lauren Blakely, NY Times Bestselling Author

* * *

Dedication

As always, there are people without whom, my books could not get written.

To Janelle Denison … for everything.

To Chasity Jenkins Patrick for knowing what I need before I need it … and for everything else.

To Shannon Short for listening and sharing your business smarts with me.

To Julie Leto and Leslie Kelly for plotting, daily help answers and more.

To Marquita Valentine for reading, cheerleading and being my daily texting buddy.

And to my Skype sprinting pals, Carrie Ann Ryan, Shayla Black, Stacey Kennedy, Kennedy Layne, Angel Payne, Lexi Blake and Jenna Jacobs for being there to sprint when I need a push – and a chat – and a pick me up. And to Mari Carr who's supposed to be there sprinting but mostly just hooked me up with this wonderful group!

You all rock and I couldn't do what I do without you. At the very least it wouldn't be as much fun! xo

Chapter One

Some women always managed to get it right. To make the right choices, to pick the right man, to nail this crazy thing called life. Meg Thompson, on the other hand, managed to end up single and pregnant. But she couldn't regret the baby growing inside her, and from now on, she was determined to get things right.

She pulled on her favorite pair of jeans, tugged them up over her hips, and unsuccessfully attempted to close the button. She grunted and lay down on the bed, pulling the sides closer together but no luck. She wriggled, sucked in a deep breath, and tried again, only to end up huffing out a stream of air in frustration.

"Didn't these fit just last weekend?" she asked herself, peeling the denim off her legs and tossing them onto the floor with a groan.

She glanced down at her still-flat stomach, placing her hand over her belly. "How could something I can't see or feel cause so much upheaval in my life?" And how could she love the baby growing inside her so much already?

A vibrating buzz told her someone was sending her a message. She checked her phone.

Lizzy: *Almost ready?*

Meg sighed. Her best friend, Elizabeth Cooper, was due to pick her up in ten minutes. Girls' night out. Or, in Lizzy's words, hookup night and Meg's last chance for a hot, no-holds-barred fling before she started to show and her sole focus became being a new mom. Meg was up for girls' night, but no way would she be picking up a stranger for a one-night stand. Her days of choosing the wrong men were over. Mike was the last in a long line of sucky choices. So not only didn't she trust her judgment when it came to the opposite sex, it no longer mattered. She was finished relying on men to define her or make her happy.

"Right, baby?" She patted her belly and headed to her closet for a pair of elastic-waist leggings.

*　　*　　*

Meg and her friends settled into their seats at Mel's, a popular spot for casual drinks after work and on the weekends. Mel's was a dimly lit bistro with a wood-fired oven and grill in the back, dark mahogany-looking tables throughout, and a funky bar where people gathered. Meg loved it here.

She waved to the waiter, who stepped over to their table.

"What can I get you ladies?"

The girls ordered alcoholic drinks, and the good-looking waiter turned to Meg.

"I'll have a club soda. With a lime."

"Going for the hard stuff, I see." He winked and scribbled down her order.

Meg smiled. "Designated driver." Which wasn't a lie. Lizzy might have picked her up, but Meg would be the one driving home.

She glanced around at the women she'd ignored for a long time in favor of her asshole ex and, unfortunately, her baby daddy. She was grateful these women were here for her now because Meg had a bad habit of dropping friends in favor of men. Men she looked to for the love and acceptance she'd never received from her own father she barely remembered. Meg sighed and rested her chin on her hands. Her childhood memories included a string of Alicia's boyfriends who came and went from her young life.

Her mother had set a pattern Meg unconsciously followed. First she'd latched on to Dylan Rhodes, the one and only good guy in her life. He'd been her high school boyfriend and her rock until they broke up before going to college, and then Meg began emulating her mother's taste by choosing men who always took advantage one way or another.

Luckily she and Dylan had reconnected when they'd moved back to Miami years later, but Meg had over-relied on Dylan instead of standing on her own two feet. It took Dylan falling hard for another woman to wake Meg up to her too-needy ways. Dylan was her friend, but he was now Olivia Dare's husband. And Meg was determined to be independent. Everything the way it should be.

"Earth to Meg." Lizzy waved a hand in front of her eyes.

Meg blinked, startled. "Sorry. Just got lost there for a minute."

"Nowhere good, from the look on your face." Lizzy tilted her head to one side, her long blonde curls falling over her shoulder. "Everything okay?" Her friend studied her, her brown eyes soft and concerned.

Meg smiled. "Couldn't be better. I was actually thinking about the changes I've made—that I'm determined to keep making in my life. And it's really good to be out with you guys," Meg said, meaning it.

"It's great to be out with you too," Lizzy said.

The waiter stopped by the table and passed out their beverages. Meg took a long sip of her cold soda, appreciating the way it eased her dry throat.

"Well, you must be doing something right because you're glowing," Lizzy said.

"It's the pregnancy hormones," Meg muttered.

"No, seriously. You look beautiful," her friend insisted.

Meg smiled at her. "Thank you."

Allie Mendez, the office secretary and the third woman in their posse, slipped her cell into her purse and leaned closer to join the conversation. "Maybe I should get myself pregnant, because Lizzy's right. You're gorgeous."

Meg blushed. "And you two need glasses."

"Not if the guys at the next table are any indication. Look. The blond one can't take his eyes off you!" Lizzy said, her voice rising in excitement.

Oh no. All Lizzy needed was a target and she'd be aiming Meg his way all night. "I'm sure he's looking at one of you. Not the pregnant woman in the elastic-waist pants." Lizzy and her blonde beauty or Allie and her olive skin and luscious curves attracted men wherever they went.

"You must not have looked in a mirror before leaving the house," Allie told her, a frown on her pretty face.

"Oh, look! He's coming this way. Now remember. There's nothing wrong with getting yourself some before your life gets serious." Lizzy nudged her arm.

"I don't want some," Meg muttered. "If he's so hot, you should—"

"Hi, ladies," the man said, bracing an arm on the back of Meg's chair.

"Hi!" Lizzy said too brightly.

"My friends and I would like to buy you all a drink." He spoke to the table, but his eyes were on Meg.

She shook her head. "We were just having a private convers—"

"We'd like that," Allie chimed in.

"Mind if we join you then?" he asked, making Meg wonder if he was dense, oblivious, or just that ego-driven.

In response, Lizzy slid her chair away from Meg, making room for the other man to sit. Which, after grabbing his chair and pulling it over to the table, he did. His pals joined them too.

Meg shot her friend an annoyed look.

"Give him a chance," Lizzy mouthed behind the man's back.

Rob, Mark, and Ken, they said their names were, as conversation began to flow. Ken was the one closest to Meg, and with his light hair and coloring, he definitely resembled his Barbie-doll namesake. Even if she were interested in a hookup, a preppy man who liked to talk about himself wouldn't be her choice. She disliked his wandering hands even more.

He brushed her back.

She stiffened.

He sat forward so their shoulders touched. She shoved her chair in the opposite direction.

Somehow he ended up close beside her again, his thigh touching hers.

She was all too ready to go home, but her friends seemed to like the guys they were talking to, and she didn't want to ruin their time by being rude to Ken. She wouldn't leave with him, but she'd be pleasant while they were here.

"So what do you do for a living?" he asked.

"I'm a kindergarten teacher."

He blinked, long lashes framing green eyes. "That's ... brave."

"Don't like kids?" she asked, none too sweetly.

He fake-shuddered. "Not for a good long while. But you must have a decent pension plan?" he asked, back on the subject he liked best. Ken was a stock-broker and investor, and soon she found herself listening to all the ways she could save more money by investing with the best of the best. Him, of course.

She hid a yawn behind her hand, and when her bladder informed her she needed a trip to the re-stroom, she nearly groaned out loud in relief.

"If you'll excuse me, I need to go ... freshen up.

I'll be back in a few minutes." Meg rose and Ken followed, helping her pull out her chair.

Allie met her gaze. "Gentleman," she mouthed in approval.

Meg swallowed a groan.

"I'll be waiting," Ken said as she walked away.

"Oh, please don't be," she said to herself, making her way to the bathroom at the far back of the restaurant.

She spent a long time in the restroom, checking her phone, swiping some gloss on her dry lips, and washing her hands, twice, in her effort to stall returning to the table.

When she did, she paused by Lizzy's chair and whispered in her friend's ear. "I'm going to bail. I'm not up to this. I'm really sorry. Will you be okay driving?"

"Of course. I barely had a sip. But I can leave and take you home."

She shook her head. "No need. You seem to be hitting it off with Mark. I can get Uber," she said of the car service in most cities, including Miami.

"I'd be happy to drive you," Ken said.

She hadn't realized he'd left his seat and had over-heard them.

"No, really. Stay and have fun. I'm just not feeling too well." Which was a lie, but it was nicer than *go away, I'm not interested.*

Which was ironic, since not too long ago, Meg would have been all too willing to see where things went with a guy who showed her any interest at all. Maybe the baby really was changing her, making her more self-reliant and aware as well as giving her better taste in men.

"Then you really shouldn't go home alone," Ken said, grasping her forearm.

Oh no, he didn't. She pinned him with an annoyed glare. "Let. Go." And what was it about her that attracted assholes anyway? she asked herself, as she tried to extricate herself without resorting to insults or calling management.

Lizzy jumped up from her seat just as the jerk released her arm, and a familiar voice reverberated in her ear.

"Touch her again and you'll answer to me."

*   *   *

Scott Dare arrived at Mel's and found his brother Tyler waiting for him at the bar. He and Tyler often hung out at Mel's on Scott's rare nights off duty. He was a cop, and after disobeying a direct order by going into a situation without backup, he was currently enjoying administrative leave. He was chafing under the rules and no longer finding the same satisfaction in the job as he once had. Meeting with his brother was the highlight of his week so far.

Scott tipped his beer back and took a long pull.

"So seriously, what's up your ass other than boredom?" Tyler asked.

"Boredom isn't enough?" Scott scanned the room, his gaze landing on a table of women he hadn't noticed before that included one very familiar face. His boredom instantly vanished.

Any time he saw Meg Thompson, every part of him took notice, and tonight was no exception. He didn't know what it was about her. Her brown hair was just that. Brown silk that hung just below her shoulders, but there were highlights that turned some parts a sexy reddish-blonde under the right light. Brown eyes the color of his morning coffee framed by thick lashes that too often showed a vulnerability she tried hard to hide. It was that forced strength that got to him. She was alone, dealing with a difficult situation that would break most women.

But she wasn't like any other woman he'd met. And completely unlike Scott's ex-wife.

"Do you know them?" Tyler tipped his head toward the table of women.

"I know the brunette." Scott rose ... only to find a blond guy had beat him to it. The man leaned closer to Meg, and Scott stiffened, forcing himself to sit down and watch.

"Who is she?" his brother asked.

"She's Dylan's friend, Meg Thompson."

"Aah. Liv told me about her. She thought Meg would be a problem when she got involved with Dylan, but they ended up being friends."

Scott nodded. "That's her."

"And I'm guessing you two have history since you can't take your eyes off of her?" Tyler nudged him in the side.

"Yes. No. Shit," he muttered, wondering how to explain his reaction to Meg.

From the minute Scott had seen her, looking small and defenseless in a hospital bed after nearly losing her baby thanks to her angry ex-boyfriend, Scott had been invested. Not even her pregnancy had put him off. Which, all things considered, should scare the shit out of him. Since Leah, he didn't get seriously involved.

He'd questioned Meg, taken her statement, and guided her through the restraining order process. And he'd been dumb enough to try and help. To be there for her afterwards, but she wasn't interested. Not in a helping hand.

Not in him. He'd been forced to see her at occasional get-togethers in the last month at Olivia and Dylan's, had run into her in the supermarket. He'd offered to take her to dinner, to be her friend. Despite the undeniable chemistry between them, she'd declined.

Two other men joined the first, and soon the women at Meg's table were paired off. And Scott was pissed. A low growl escaped his throat.

"Easy, bro." Instead of giving him a hard time, Tyler placed a hand on his shoulder.

Scott blew out a long breath. Logically, he knew he didn't have a say in what Meg did. Or with whom.

He ordered a Patron. Neat. And settled in to do what he did best. Keep an eye on her from a distance. To his relief, as time passed, she didn't look at all interested in the guy. Her body language screamed *don't touch*, and the asshole didn't appear to be listening.

"I'm going to bash his head in if this keeps up," Scott muttered.

Tyler raised an eyebrow. "First Ian, now you. Are you really going to leave me as the only single Dare guy in the family?"

"She's made it clear she's not interested in me, and besides, marriage? Been there, have the divorce papers to show for it. Not happening again," Scott reminded his brother. At twenty-nine, he was finished with that stupid dream. Leah had screwed with his head on so many levels he was lucky he wasn't still dizzy two years later.

He had no intention of letting his brother in on the

fact that Meg was pregnant. His sibling would have a field day with Scott's interest based on that alone. He'd be wrong. But it wasn't worth the hassle or discussion.

"Sorry," Tyler muttered, obviously uncomfortable.

Scott wasn't sure if he was referring to the divorce, the reason behind it, or Meg's lack of interest. All were enough to shit on his ego.

Meg shoved her chair back and headed for the back of the restaurant, where the restrooms were located, and Scott breathed easily for the first time since realizing she was here.

"You going after her?" Tyler asked.

"No."

"It's not like you to give up when you want something."

Good point, Scott thought, but he remained seated. Watching but wary.

Meg returned and stopped by one of her friends, whispering something in her ear. The women spoke, and suddenly the guy who'd been inching closer to her all evening walked up to them. They talked. Looked more like an argument.

And then he grabbed Meg's arm. Scott bolted out of his seat and came up behind Meg. Her soft scent invaded his senses, but his focus was on the asshole who hadn't released her.

"Let. Go," Meg said through clenched teeth.

Scott's hands fisted at his sides. "Touch her again and you'll answer to me."

*   *   *

Meg didn't know where Scott Dare had come from. She hadn't noticed him in the bar earlier, and she was always aware when he was near. How could she not be? He was everything that appealed to her in a man. Tall with jet-black hair that always looked as if he'd just run his hand through the inky strands. Full lips. Straight nose. So damned handsome.

Though he had a dominant streak a mile wide, one she couldn't miss during their few encounters, he'd been warm and caring when taking her statement in the hospital. And he was a cop, which meant he wasn't her typical bad boy, but he gave off a masculine vibe that just did it for her.

"Who the hell are you?" Ken asked Scott, interrupting her blatant perusal.

"A friend who heard her tell you to get lost." If Scott's pissed-off tone and much bigger build wasn't enough to make his point, he pushed his jacket back, revealing his holstered gun. "I'm off duty but it still works."

Ken raised both hands and took a step back. "Easy, man. It's not my fault she gave off the wrong signals." He shook his head and stormed off, his friends pushing their chairs back and quickly following.

"Are you okay?" Lizzy asked, her hand protectively on Meg's arm.

"I'm fine."

"And who is this?" Allie asked, coming up on Meg's other side.

She tipped her head toward Scott, still not meeting his gaze. She wasn't ready. "Liz, Allie, this is Scott Dare."

"Holy hell, girl," Allie whispered none too softly. "I can see why you weren't interested in the Ken doll."

Meg's cheeks burned.

"Nice to meet you both," he said in that voice that Meg heard in her dreams.

He turned toward her, giving her no choice but to look into those sexy navy—almost violet—eyes, made more vibrant by his light blue shirt. "Meg, a word?"

She shook her head. She'd managed to put him out of her thoughts, which hadn't been easy, and here he was, coming to her rescue and making demands. If she wasn't so determined to turn over a new leaf, be independent, she'd respond to his sexy tone and probably do anything he asked. Her damp panties were proof of that.

"I was just telling my friends I'm going home." She kissed Lizzy on the cheek and squeezed Allie's hand, reassuring them both she was fine.

She strode past Scott knowing full well he'd follow. He waited until they were on the street away from the crowds before he grasped her hand and turned her to face him. "Meg."

"Thank you for getting rid of the creep." She pulled her phone from her bag and scrolled for the app that would let her call for a car.

He caught her wrist. "I'll drive you home."

"Was that an offer or an order?" she asked, unable to help her sarcastic mouth. He brought that out in her.

He shot her a look. One that had her quivering inside. And giving in to his demand. "Okay, you can drive me home."

And then she planned to walk herself inside, close her front door, and forget about Scott Dare.

Without a word, he grasped her elbow and led her to a parking lot where his Range Rover was parked.

"I can't believe what a mess tonight turned out to be," she muttered once they were settled in the plush leather seats.

"What were you doing there in the first place?"

She swung around to face him. "I can't go out to a restaurant with friends?"

"Of course you can."

He wanted to say more. She could tell from the

tense set of his jaw.

She sighed and decided to save him the trouble. "No, you're right. Lizzy and Allie had this idea of taking me out so I could pick up a guy and have one last fling before I start to show." She slid her hands over her stomach. "And before I'm busy being a mom."

His grip on the steering wheel tightened. "You were going to hook up with some stranger?" he asked through gritted teeth.

"What? No! I said they thought I should. I just went out to see my friends. Then that guy sat down and—Why am I explaining myself to you?" she asked, trailing off.

But it had been this way with Scott, from the first time they'd met. She found him easy to talk to. Understanding. Like he heard what she said and cared, unlike her ex. Or any of the men in her past.

She watched the palm trees and scenery as he drove. She'd already told him where she lived when she'd explained how she'd ended up in the hospital a little over a month ago. She just couldn't believe he remembered. All too soon, they reached their destination. He pulled into a parking spot at her apartment complex.

He put the truck in park, cut the engine, and turned to face her. "You talk to me because you know that you can trust me."

Point proven. He remembered what she'd said at least five minutes ago.

"But I hardly know you."

"Instinct."

She shook her head at that. "Mine's failed me many times before." And miserably, at that, she thought.

"Not this time." He let himself out of the truck and started to walk around to her side.

Realizing his intent, she opened the door and hopped out just as he reached her. He shut the door behind her. "Let's go."

"I can see myself up."

"You could. But since I took you home, I'll get you safely to your door."

He slid a hand to the small of her back, and she felt his heated palm through the fabric of her top. Goose bumps prickled along her skin.

She lived in a first-floor apartment, and they reached her door. He turned her around to face him. "Your friends want you to have one last fling? Is that what you want too?"

She hadn't given a fling any thought. Not until Scott said the word, a husky bent to his voice and determined intent behind his words. "I don't want sex with some random stranger."

She glanced up and found herself pinned by his stare. His lips lifted in a sexy grin. "I'm not a stranger."

She opened then closed her mouth as she processed his words and the meaning behind them. He wasn't a stranger. Not really. He knew more about her than most people, and her best friends could vouch for him.

She ran her tongue over her dry lips. His darkening gaze deliberately followed the movement, and her body responded, nipples puckering beneath the cotton of her shirt. He wanted a fling. Sex. With her.

And she wanted him, every rock-hard inch of his toned, muscled body. Had from the very first moment she'd seen him, and every time since. She'd evaded him, certain that was the right thing to do for herself and for her baby, because she had new standards and rules she had to follow for her own sanity and for her future. But this *thing* between them wasn't going away. If anything, it was becoming more intense, growing more heated, and she couldn't deny it or walk away from him again.

"I'm not interested in a relationship," she reminded him.

He inclined his head. "And I'm not asking for one. Not even asking for a date this time."

"Just a fling?" she repeated, thinking he had to be kidding. Just like she'd thought he was kidding when he'd asked her out before. Because what would a hot, good-looking man like Scott Dare want with a woman who'd gotten herself knocked up and then pushed around by her ex-boyfriend?

Even when she'd realized Scott was serious about dating, she couldn't accept. Because she could so easily see herself repeating old patterns with him. Falling hard and fast. Giving in. Losing herself. And now there was more at stake than just Meg.

But this time, Scott was offering something she could handle. A night with a beginning and an end, no expectations. No disturbing her resolution to stand on her own. To be a better mother than her own had been, no revolving door of men. No man, period. Just a hot night and a memory to keep her warm when she was alone.

"One night." He reached out and rubbed his thumb across her lower lip.

His touch made her tremble, and her nipples tightened into hardened points, and the intensity in his gorgeous eyes had need building even stronger inside her.

"Is that what you want too?" he asked again, his gaze hot on hers.

His distinctive scent, a hint of musk she associated with Scott alone, filled her nostrils. Her stomach fluttered, and the desire to wrap herself around him and take what he offered built until it was a tangible thing, living and breathing inside her tightly strung body.

She nodded, unable to speak. Her throat had grown too dry.

"I need you to say it."

Say what? She didn't remember his question. Only the thought of letting him into her apartment ... into her body filled her mind and her senses.

A low rumble sounded from deep inside his chest. "Say *I want you, Scott.* I need the words or I'll send you inside alone."

"I want you, Scott." The words tumbled out, an easy capitulation that had been anything but. Another Meg Thompson decision she feared would alter the course of her life. And she was powerless to stop it.

Chapter Two

Meg said the words, and Scott's head buzzed with her heady admission. He'd been holding on by a thread since she'd admitted that her friends wanted her to have a one-night stand. If anyone was going to put hands on her, it was going to be him. Problem was, once he touched her … once he *had* her, one time wouldn't be enough. But that was an issue he'd deal with later.

She opened the door to her apartment. They stepped inside, and he immediately pressed her up against the wall, his hips bracing against hers. "I want you too. And if this is what you'll give me, I'm taking it."

He leaned close, intending to kiss her, but her scent beckoned, and he breathed in the warm, sensual fragrance that made him hard and kept him up nights.

He dragged his lips from her jaw to her cheek. "You smell so fucking good."

A small whimper escaped from the back of her throat, and his dick hardened against the teeth of his zipper.

"I need to taste you." He settled his mouth over hers, finding her lips soft, her flavor sweet. Better than he'd imagined, and he wanted more. He nipped at her lower lip and slid his tongue inside, turning things hot quickly.

He discovered Meg was an equal partner in the glide and tangle of their tongues, in the click of his teeth against hers.

She threaded her hands through his hair and tugged, and he knew if she kept touching him, it'd be over before things got started. He pulled her arms above her head and clasped her wrists in one hand. "I call the shots."

He watched her carefully and her eyes dilated. He grinned, liking her response. He'd always preferred control, more so after his marriage and life had fallen apart, and his older brother Ian had taught him not to apologize for who he was or what he needed. His cousin Decklan had introduced him to his favorite club in New York, and Scott had begun to understand himself even more.

"I'm not sure I like that," she said, her mind obviously at war with what her needy body craved.

"When I make you come over and over, you will."

Her eyes opened wide. And then she laughed. Damned woman actually laughed at him. He raised an eyebrow.

"What?" she asked, her eyes lighting up. "Experience tells me that was a cocky claim."

"You did not just call my skill into question."

She met his gaze, a combination of mirth and seriousness in her chocolate-brown eyes. "Maybe it's the skill of all those men in my past I'm talking about," she murmured, her voice dropping, honesty and embarrassment forcing her gaze down.

Olivia had told him Meg had a history of picking the wrong guys. A pattern that went far beyond the asshole who'd laid a hand on her this last time. Now Scott understood just how bad her prior relationships had been, and he intended to make up for each and every jerk in her past. Something that would take way more than one night.

But he'd start now. "Okay, baby, I'm going to lay down a few rules."

Her mouth opened and closed.

So damned cute, but he wouldn't tell her that.

"I am not your baby," she said, but the gleam in her eyes told him otherwise. She liked when he called her that.

He grinned. "We'll see."

She narrowed her gaze. "And did you say *rules*?"

Meg asked, unable to believe his nerve.

He nodded. "Rules. As in, you do as I say and you get to come. Often."

How could she argue with that? Before she could even respond, he picked her up and into his arms, enjoying the warmth of her body against his. "Direct me to the bedroom."

"Are you always this bossy?" she asked. And why oh why did her pussy spasm when he acted like this? A normal woman would be turned off, but not Meg. A guy took control and she wanted more.

"Yes. Get used to it. Back there?" he tilted his head toward the open doorway and, without waiting for an answer, strode to her room.

He paused by the bed, dipped his head, and kissed her hard. This was no first-date kiss, but then this wasn't a date. This was sex, and she already knew it was going to be the best she'd ever had.

It might also be the last, so she'd better enjoy it. She wrapped her arms around his neck, her fingers gliding over the hard muscles in his upper back, which she could feel through his clothing, then up through his silky hair. She inhaled, and his masculine scent raced through her, a heady reminder she really was doing this. With Scott, a man she'd wanted since meeting him, she thought, and her belly twisted with need.

He laid her down on the center of the bed, his movements sure and gentler than she'd expected. Then he rose. He removed his jacket and tossed it onto the floor, took care of the holstered gun, placing it on the dresser—and boy, did she find a man with a weapon hot. Especially this man. She couldn't stop staring as he yanked his shirt up and off, revealing tanned skin and a light sprinkling of dark hair across his chest that ran down his abs and tapered into the waistband of his jeans.

He was a sculpted work of art, and she watched him greedily. Ran her tongue over her lips.

"I want that tongue on me, baby."

She couldn't believe the calm, collected, always-in-control Scott Dare was a dirty talker during sex, and her stomach flipped in excitement at his words. She wanted her tongue on him too. She, who could normally care less about oral sex, wanted to take him in her mouth and lick him all over.

"So come here and let me," she said, shocked at the gravelly tone of her voice.

His gaze narrowed. "Who calls the shots?" he asked, unbuttoning his jeans and pulling them down over narrow hips. He'd hooked his thumbs into his boxers or briefs, she didn't know which because they were gone along with his jeans and she couldn't tear her gaze away from his thick, hard cock.

Jesus.

"Was that an answer?" he asked.

Had he asked a question? Her breasts were heavy, her nipples hard and hurting, and her panties now soaked with the evidence of her desire for him. And she was lying in bed, fully dressed while this gorgeous specimen of a man stood aroused before her. She couldn't focus on anything but getting naked too.

She reached for the hem of her shirt, and suddenly he was over her, pinning her to the bed. "You can't deny me the pleasure of peeling those clothes off you. I want to see every inch of your skin."

He lifted the shirt and eased it upward, his calloused thumbs trailing over her sensitive flesh. He pulled it off, leaving her in just a flimsy bra, one that would have to be replaced soon, because it did little to conceal the now-larger swells of her breasts.

His gaze never left her body, his eyes darkening as he drank her in. "You're gorgeous."

He swiped his thumbs over her already-aching nipples, and she moaned, his words arousing her as much as his touch. He trailed his fingertips down, then slid his hand into the waistband of her leggings and soon removed those too. Of course, he took her panties along with them in one smooth move.

As he continued to stare, she wanted to crawl beneath the covers, suddenly aware of herself in ways she hadn't been when focused on him. Her breasts were bigger now, and although she figured that was okay, her stomach wasn't flat and tight. She'd always had a slight belly, but everything had shifted lately, making her overly focused on her flaws.

No way he hadn't noticed them too. She slid her hands over her stomach, and he swore, grasping her wrists and pinning them over her head.

"Let's get something straight, okay? I'm here because I want you. All of you. From what's inside that pretty head of yours to the sexy body spread out for me now."

Her eyes widened at the force and sincerity of his words.

"Know what that means?" he asked.

She shook her head. She didn't know anything. This man had her so off-balance she was spinning. She'd agreed to one night of hot sex. Instead, she was getting a lot of dirty talking and attentive man. She didn't know what to do with either.

"That means while I have you in bed, you're mine." He nipped her jaw, then kissed her hard on the lips. "Keep your hands above your head and let me give you what you need."

"Again, you seem awfully sure of yourself," she said, falling back on sarcasm. Because what could she say? She was so out of her depth.

A knowing grin pulled at his lips. "Guess you're going to make me prove myself, huh?"

Her mouth grew dry. "Guess so."

He proceeded to do just that. He kissed, licked, and nipped his way down her neck, pausing to nuzzle at her collarbone, an erogenous spot she hadn't known she possessed, before licking around the lace edges of her bra. Her nerves tingled, the rest of her becoming increasingly aroused, and she writhed and twisted on the bed, arms above her head, with him effectively holding her hostage. She didn't care as long as he continued to pay homage to her body.

He unhooked the front catch of her bra with way too much skill and peeled the cups off her heavy breasts. "I need to taste you, baby."

Her sex clenched. Her nipples peaked even tighter. And when he latched on to one sensitive tip, she felt the tug deep in her core. "Scott, God." She arched up, inadvertently pushing her breast deeper into his mouth.

He cupped one big hand around her other breast and began to pluck and play with the nipple, pulling and pinching with his fingers, his mouth continuing to do the same with the other tip. Sensations pummeled her and rocked her hips back and forth, her pussy seeking the same rough, hard contact he was giving to her breasts.

He pinched a nipple harder and she whimpered.

"You're sensitive, aren't you?"

She nodded. "That's sort of … new. I never—" But she was so close. Could she really come from him playing with her breasts alone?

"You will now." He followed that comment by lavishing her with the most wonderful tugs, pulls, and twists of his fingers and wet laps of his tongue.

As if he'd tapped into a powder keg, sparks flew from her nipples to her clit, a dull roar filled her head, and suddenly he slid his fingers over her sex, adding to the maelstrom. The sounds surrounding her were unfamiliar, loud, and she realized, coming from her. He slid two fingers back and forth over her clit, the pressure building and making her ready to detonate.

"Come, baby."

His words triggered the explosion, and her body began to pulse and fly, her orgasm a living, breathing thing that consumed her, body and soul. The waves of pleasure went on and on with Scott in control, his rough voice and slick fingers taking her on a glorious ride.

She came back to herself as he braced his hands on either side of her shoulders, his large body over hers. "Good?" he asked.

Her lips lifted in what had to be a loopy grin. "Yes, hotshot. You proved you're a man of your word."

"Not yet, I haven't." His gaze met hers, that pene-trating stare zeroing in. "I promised you'd come often. That was just once." He slid his erection back and forth over her sex, and what little breath she'd regained left in a whoosh.

"Condom."

She swallowed hard. "I think there are some left in my drawer." She looked away.

He pressed a hard kiss to her lips, retrieved protec-tion, ripped the foil open, and slid it on. "I need to feel you wet and hot around my cock." He rocked his thick member lower, nudging at her entrance, gliding in, pulling out with short thrusts and rough groans. Back and forth with obvious care.

She had the distinct feeling he was going slowly in deference to her, and that was the last thing she wanted. "I'm not going to break," she told him.

He studied her as if searching for answers, his need obvious in his taut expression. He was holding back.

"The doctor didn't give me any restrictions." She arched her hips and clasped him more tightly inside her, drawing her knees up and pulling him in deeper.

With a groan, he broke and thrust hard, filling her up completely. He was so big, and she reveled in the fullness. She wrapped her arms around him, and he didn't stop her from touching him this time, so she took the time to memorize the moment. The way his hard body molded to hers, the thickness of him inside her, and his heady, arousing scent. She didn't want to forget a second of this moment and knew she never would.

"Can't not move," he muttered and began a steady pounding inside her, giving her everything, holding nothing back.

His body felt glorious inside hers, and to her shock, pleasure began to tease her again, another climax building quickly. He took her hard, his thrusts culminating with a grind of his hips, the angle of his penetration hitting a spot she'd never known existed but was sheer bliss. Sweat broke out on his body, and his rough groans sounded in her ear.

"Fuck, you feel good," he said as his lips came down on hers, his deliberate thrusts never ceasing. "Meg!" He groaned and slammed into her over and over, his release obvious and so hot it triggered her own. Soaring again, she came, her entire being narrowing to the epic sensations pouring over her and the man atop her who'd rocked her world.

She was still breathing hard when Scott pulled out and headed for the bathroom. He returned seconds later, wasting no time in gathering her into his arms and throwing one big leg over hers.

Was he planning on *staying?* she wondered, panicked. That wasn't what they'd agreed on. She'd enjoyed him too much and would come to want so much more if he didn't get up and leave now. So she lay stiff in his arms, unsure of what to say or do next.

Scott apparently had no such qualms. He kissed her neck, soft, sexy slides of his mouth that had her squirming because she liked them so much.

"Relax, baby," he said drowsily. "The world won't end if I fall asleep here." And from the lazy drawl of his words, he intended to do just that.

* * *

Scott awoke in a strange bed, loud sounds coming from the other room. He was in Meg's bedroom. He grinned and stretched, feeling too damned pleased considering that, without a doubt, she wanted him gone. He understood the sentiment. They'd agreed on hot sex and nothing more. Of course he'd had a hunch he wouldn't be satisfied with just one night, and in the bright light of day, he'd been right. He didn't understand why he wanted to get entangled with a woman whose life was damned complicated. Given his history, it made little sense. But right now he was in. He'd figure out his own issues later.

He headed for the bathroom, discovering it steamy. Meg had obviously already showered and dressed, no doubt steeling herself for the confrontation ahead. He shrugged. He'd just have to keep her off-balance if he wanted to break through her walls.

He took a quick shower of his own, lathering in her soap, using her shampoo. Both smells made him hard, but he was well aware he wasn't getting any this morning. He just needed to assess the lay of the land for the future before heading out.

Dressed in his clothes from yesterday, he found her in the kitchen, her back to the door. She wore a pair of sweats and a pale green tee shirt, her damp hair hanging long in the back, curling as it dried.

"Good morning."

She jumped and turned toward him. "You startled me."

"Is that breakfast?" He pointed to a pink smoothie she drank from a straw.

She nodded. "Protein. It's good for me."

"And the baby. I didn't forget." One of her many complications. He pushed the reality away.

A light blush stained her cheeks. "Right. So you understand why we shouldn't draw out this awkward morning-after thing any longer."

He raised an eyebrow. So she really was eager to get rid of him, and it rankled. "No breakfast?" he asked, teasing her.

"Sorry. Nothing but healthy shakes, and I really need to get my day going so…" She gestured toward the front of her apartment.

He strode toward her, leaning one hip against the kitchen counter. "About last night." He slid one hand behind her neck in a possessive hold.

"What about it?" she asked, voice shaking. She didn't know what to expect from him, but he affected her. Her body and voice couldn't lie about that.

"It was great," he told her honestly. "*You* were great." He touched his nose to hers in a soft gesture, one he knew was at odds with the man he was in the bedroom. But she brought this side out in him too. Something else to ponder, as nobody ever had before. "So thank you."

"Oh. You're welcome." She blushed harder. "I mean … never mind." She waved a shaking hand through the air.

There it was. Cute again. He shook his head, remembering his cool, icy, sophisticated ex-wife. So. Not. Cute.

He grinned at a flustered Meg. "I know what you meant."

"Oh," Meg said softly, and she slid her tongue across her lip in that nervous gesture he found so endearing.

This morning it reminded him of the things they hadn't done together. His mouth on her pussy. Her lips on his cock. Yeah, there was a lot left undone. And he wasn't just talking about sex, though that had been a good start. It would make it that much more difficult for her to keep him at arm's length now that she knew what he did. Together they were explosive.

How they came together? That would be the next step. One that would determine just what they could mean to each other outside of the bedroom.

He pulled back and rose to his full height. "Take care of yourself." Knowing she'd say no and get defensive, he didn't ask her for anything. Offer her dinner. Ask her questions. Nothing.

Keep her frustrated and guessing. Missing him, if he was lucky. That was his game plan, and he was looking forward to the challenge. Because he fully expected Meg to make him work for her. And after last night, he was okay with that.

*   *   *

Meg wasn't sure how she made it through the rest of the weekend. She was jumpy and nervous. She kept checking her phone, hoping, expecting to hear from Scott. She didn't. Apparently he was a man of his word. One night meant just that.

Wasn't that what she'd wanted? Why was she so ... hurt, then, over his silence?

Monday at school dragged. The kids were extra cranky, little Billy Miller spilled paint on Lilah Devlin's shoes, one kid had a fever, and by the time the day ended, Meg was so grateful she wanted to cry. Tomorrow she had an appointment with the principal to tell him she was pregnant. She was due in early September, when school would just have restarted for the new year, and he'd need to plan ahead. She didn't think being unmarried and pregnant would be an issue, but she was nervous anyway because she worked in a private school, and that meant she was subject to the school board's decisions, and she had no doubt the principal would share her new status with them.

On Wednesday, she was having dinner with Olivia. Dylan was out of town on business, and the other woman wanted to compare pregnancy notes. Since Olivia was due two months later than Meg, they had that in common. She hoped it wasn't awkward that Olivia was Scott's sister.

Because there was no way she could hide her reaction if somehow his name came up. Just thinking about him set her on fire. She hadn't washed her sheets because she liked the musky smell of him, and *them*, that lingered. She'd like to say it was the sex she couldn't get out of her head, but it was more than that. The little things. How he'd jumped out to open the car door. How he'd leaned in and brushed his nose against hers when he was saying good-bye. And how he'd thanked her, as if her sleeping with him was something special and meant something to him.

When was the last time she'd been treated well? When the person she'd been with had put her first? She shook her head hard, the answer too painful to contemplate. True, Scott had been nice, but he wasn't anything to her but a one-night stand. His silence merely reinforced that. Meanwhile, she had a busy week, a full life, and she had to remember that she did not need a man to make her complete.

*   *   *

At the end of a long week, Scott met his brother Tyler at the gym of the Thunder football stadium. The whole family gravitated here, to the everlasting irritation of their father, who had given them all free gym passes at his luxury hotel downtown. Scott, like the others, didn't want much to do with the old man. In fact, his becoming a cop had been a big F.U. to his dad and his offer to work in his hotel business. Scott couldn't be in business with a man he didn't respect, and from the minute he'd realized the truth about his father's cheating and other family, any respect he'd hung on to for a man who was rarely around when he was growing up had disappeared.

His grandparents had left each kid a trust fund, and money hadn't been an issue. He was luckier than most in that he could do what he wanted in life. So he'd gravitated toward law enforcement because there were rules, laws, and things were black and white. He knew what to expect. He'd never envisioned feeling constrained by those same rules, because after the personal upheaval his father had caused, his career choice had made sense to him at the time. Unfortunately, those restrictions chafed, and he was miserable.

He and Tyler worked out in silence for over an hour, then showered and were finishing up in the locker room. As it was March, the team wasn't around, and they pretty much had the place to themselves.

"I wanted to ask you something," Tyler said. "Couldn't do it the other night. Mel's is too crowded. And you were too busy looking at that brunette. What did you say her name was?"

"Meg." Scott's brain immediately filled with memories of the night with her, causing his cock to swell. Shit. Good thing he'd put his jeans on.

"Right. Meg Thompson. You get her home okay?" Tyler asked.

Scott nodded, unwilling to get into more about his relationship ... or lack thereof, with Meg. Knowing how completely freaked out she'd been the morning after, he'd given her space this week ... but he couldn't let the silence go on much longer. He didn't want her thinking he wasn't interested any more than he wanted to crowd her and send her running. Not to mention, he couldn't stop thinking about her and that hot night.

He and Tyler headed out to the hallway, pausing by a set of oversized couches in a lounge area.

"What's on your mind?" Scott asked his brother.

"I got a call from someone in the music business looking to hire us for the whole nine yards. Updated alarm systems, personal protection, you name it. Apparently a big band is considering breaking up, and someone leaked the information to the press, and they're getting angry fan threats."

Tyler ran a security company named Double Down, specializing in various areas of protection, including investigations, electronics, and personal protection. He had a group of ex-military men working for him, and he'd done well for himself.

Scott glanced at his brother. "Well, they came to the right place," he said, as always, proud of what Tyler had accomplished.

"Who is the client?"

Tyler eyed him warily. "Lola Corbin called. She's the lead singer of Tangled Royal," he said of the huge band currently rocking the music scene.

"Son of a bitch. Grey Kingston's band mate is looking to hire you?" he asked of the band's lead guitarist.

Tyler clenched his jaw and nodded.

Now Scott understood the problem. Avery, their

youngest sister, and Grey Kingston had been hot and heavy back in high school … until Grey had left town to make it big, leaving Avery heartbroken. To this day, Scott wasn't sure she'd ever gotten over it. His hands curled into fists at the thought of dealing with the man.

"At least it's not Kingston who wants your services, but that's pretty close for comfort."

Tyler ran a hand through his dark hair and nodded. "Agreed. I don't want to upset Avery but I can't turn down the biggest rock star on the planet. Not to mention, Lola Corbin is engaged to Rep Grissom, Jr., one of the Thunder's hottest stars."

"Shit," Scott muttered.

"You got that right."

"Hey, guys," Olivia said, joining her brothers. Her office was nearby. "I couldn't help but overhear. You should know, Avery's seen Grey recently. He sent her tickets to the last concert."

Tyler glanced at his sister. "Seriously? What the hell? Why didn't I know about this?"

Scott wanted to know the same thing.

"Because of your reactions right now. She knew you'd go all big-brother caveman on his ass." Olivia patted Tyler's cheek. "She asked me to go with her to the concert. We went; Dylan and I got the call about Meg being in the hospital. I offered to stay, but Avery

42

swore she was fine to go backstage alone."

"What happened between them?" Scott asked.

"She won't talk about it," Olivia said, her tone indicating how unhappy that made her.

Scott didn't like it either. Avery and Olivia were close. If she wasn't confiding in her sister, something big was going on.

"Do you think the bastard is pushing Lola towards my business to get back into Avery's life somehow?" Tyler asked, shaking his head in disgust.

Olivia narrowed her eyes, remaining silent while she considered. Then she shook her head. "You're the best there is. I honestly doubt it. She probably really does need your services."

Tyler blew out a frustrated breath. "That's what I wanted to talk about. I need you," he said to Scott. "I need a second-in-command. Someone who can oversee everything that goes on. Actually, I need a partner. I need you," he said, turning to Scott.

"What?"

"You're a damned good cop, and the beat is a waste of your talents. Not to mention, you're bored as shit. I want you to sign on as my partner." Tyler pinned Scott with a look he'd never seen before. One that held admiration and something more.

"Cool!" Olivia said, clapping her hands. "That's great for you, Scott, and he's right. You need something more challenging, and this is it."

"We all know you aren't happy doing the cop thing. This will give you a chance to use your people skills and your training. Plus you can set your own hours, which has to be better than those night shifts you've been assigned."

He couldn't deny they were right. He wasn't happy, and the thought of doing something different definitely appealed to him, as did working with his brother.

Scott ran a hand over his eyes. He'd never considered leaving the force. Never thought his older brother—by two years but still older—would want him on board. "You built your business yourself. Are you sure—"

"One hundred percent certain. You can buy in, and we can work out the details… I'd have asked you before, but I wanted you to get hands-on experience first. You deserved to follow your dream and see if it was for you before I asked you to leave it behind."

Scott nodded slowly. "Let me give it some thought. But I'm interested."

"Not too long. I'm going to take this job and with the business growing, I need you. As far as Greyson… If he shows up around Lola, we can tag-team him," Tyler said, tacking it on as added incentive.

"Oh, you two better stay out of Avery's business,"

Olivia warned them.

They both shot her a look. If someone hurt either woman, they'd have to answer to a Dare brother.

"I've got to get going. Call me," Tyler said to Scott. He paused to kiss Olivia on the cheek. "You feeling okay?" he asked their pregnant sister.

That was something Scott hadn't wrapped his head around. His baby sister married and expecting a baby. At least her husband, Dylan Rhodes, treated her right. Now to get someone decent for Avery.

Olivia poked Scott in the arm. "You and I need to talk. Come to my office?" she asked.

He rose and grinned. "Am I in trouble?"

She pinned him with a warning look. Uh oh.

She waited until they were settled in her private office, she in the chair behind her desk, he in the one in front. "What's up, Liv?"

"That's what I want to know. I had dinner with Meg. I mentioned your name, and she said she ran into you at Mel's this weekend."

"And?" He stared at his sister, not knowing where she was going, and not jumping in with anything more before he knew what had her so on edge.

"You spent the night with her!" Olivia said it like an accusation.

Scott folded his arms across his chest. "She told you that?" Because Meg didn't strike him as the gossipy type.

Olivia blew out a long breath. "Not in so many words. But I could tell from the hemming and hawing she did … from the way she blushed and couldn't look me in the eye, then asked selective questions … I just knew."

He inclined his head. "And?" he asked his nosey sister.

"And what were you thinking? I know there were sparks when you met her, but she's coming off a really shitty relationship, she's pregnant and vulnerable, and you're…" She trailed off, her gaze darting away from his.

He stiffened. "Don't stop now," he told her.

"You're *you*! All controlling and alpha."

"So you think I'd hurt her?" he asked, offended.

Olivia wrinkled her nose. "Of course not. Well, not on purpose, anyway."

He frowned. "Thanks for the vote of confidence."

She rose from her seat and came around her desk, sitting in the chair next to him and leaning in close. "Scott, do you remember what happened with Leah? She gutted you when she had that abortion. You haven't had any kind of relationship with a woman since." Olivia held up a hand to make sure he didn't interrupt. "And I'm not talking about sex."

"Me neither and not with you," Scott muttered.

Nor did he need the reminder of how wrong he'd chosen when he'd married Leah Jerome.

Having seen firsthand what his father's cheating had done, not only to his mother but to him and his siblings, Scott hadn't believed he wanted a family. Leah definitely hadn't. And then she'd gotten pregnant ... and the reality of a baby had changed his mind. He'd thought he could change hers. He'd been wrong. And Olivia was correct. He hadn't trusted another woman since.

Then he'd met Meg. "I'm not going to hurt her. You know me better than that."

"Of course I do." Olivia laid a hand on his arm. "But all your women lately have been one-night stands or close to it. I don't understand how you can cavalierly sleep with a pregnant woman and walk away. Or think it's okay to have an affair with her like she's just a woman you picked up in a bar."

"Whoa." This time he held up his hand. "I'm not sure where you're getting these ideas, but trust me, Liv, you have no clue what I'm thinking, feeling, or planning." Unfortunately, neither did he. But it was the early days... They'd slept together once. And he wasn't going to let his sister convince him to walk away.

His sister narrowed her gaze. "Care to share?"

"Not particularly. Just understand, you know who

I am. That should count for something."

"I know," Olivia said, her voice softening. "You're a good man. But Meg is different than the women you're used to."

He knew that. She was everything his ex wasn't. He sensed it at a glance. All those differences—the softness beneath the prickly exterior, the outward fragility that he knew belied a strong core, and the beauty that shone from her inside and out all called to a part of him he'd never known before.

"She has a history of picking bad boys who aren't good to her, and she's just promised herself she'll change."

"And you think I'm going to stop her from doing that?"

"I know you *could*."

He ran a hand over his face. Yeah … he could. It was in his nature to take over, to control. He wanted to help her, take care of her and get to know her better. But contrary to what his sister believed, he wouldn't hurt her. He meant to see what could be between them. If that meant pushing her past her limits … he'd do just that.

Chapter Three

Meg had a rough week. The meeting with the principal hadn't gone as she'd hoped. Although she had a morals clause in her contract, it didn't include having a child out of wedlock, and she'd counted on her abilities as a teacher and how much the kids loved her to hold sway. So she'd be a single parent. Women handled it all the time due to divorce or death. They also, occasionally, got themselves pregnant.

Unfortunately, Mr. Ryan Hansen hadn't been happy. Meg wasn't sure if his censure was more because he'd tried to date her before or because he really did have an issue with her teaching children and having to explain to young, impressionable minds why there was no baby daddy in her life. As if a kindergartener would even know about her personal life, let alone think to ask.

Luckily, he couldn't get rid of her. She had just

signed a new contract, and she hoped her job was secure … if no longer comfortable. She blew out a breath, knowing she had to get used to people having opinions and comments about her situation.

Meg settled into the couch in her apartment, laptop on her thighs, the television providing background noise. She drew a deep breath and began looking for baby items at online stores, making notes on a pad at her side. Budget was important, but safety was first. If she needed to deal with credit card debt to purchase what she needed for her baby, so be it. She had things she could easily give up to free up money. Professional haircuts, eyebrow waxing, mani-pedis, all things she could manage on her own.

A crib would be the biggest hit for now. She jotted down a few possibilities and prices. She didn't want to go into stores until she had a good idea what she could afford.

Her doorbell rang, taking her by surprise. It was Friday night, and her friends had gone out for drinks. They'd invited her, but she'd begged off, wanting a quiet night at home.

She walked to the door, placed her hand on the knob. "Who is it?"

She was just about to look through the peephole when she heard, "Open the fucking door, Meg."

Her heart skipped a beat.

Mike?

How could he dare show up here? She had a restraining order in effect. She didn't plan on answering him or letting him inside, but she couldn't stop the tremors that took hold. Shaking, she went back to the couch and picked up her cell.

She returned to the door and leaned against it, hoping he would go away.

He banged hard again. No doorbell this time. "Meg! We need to talk."

She drew a deep breath. He could talk to her lawyer, and he knew it. All she wanted was for him to sign away rights to the baby. For whatever reason, he refused to do it. She didn't have any illusions that he wanted the baby. He just didn't want the child to exist, period.

She placed a protective hand over her stomach. "Go away or I'll call the police." What the hell had she seen in him? How had she missed this side of him? Oh, he'd been fun and exciting ... at first. Until she'd let him move in and he hadn't paid rent. He hadn't contributed to food. And he'd done what he wanted, when he wanted. And she'd still tried to make things work because it was easier than getting him out of the apartment. Easier than fighting all the time. Just like her mother's relationships.

Ugh.

"Come on, I just want to talk." He banged harder on the door.

"I'm dialing 911!"

She lifted the phone.

"You stupid bitch!" He slammed his hand against the door, and then she heard the sound of footsteps storming down the hall. She wondered what her neighbors thought. It wasn't the first time they'd heard screaming coming from her apartment. She cringed in embarrassment.

She was still shaking, and there was nothing she could do to calm down. She couldn't pour herself a glass of wine. She couldn't take a Xanax. She just had to deal.

She lowered herself back to the couch and drew in a deep breath. She wasn't sure how long she remained motionless, seeing nothing, doing nothing but shivering. The last time she'd seen Mike, she'd told him she was pregnant … and he'd been angry. She still didn't think he'd deliberately pushed her, but who knew?

She'd tripped and fallen back into the curio cabinet with all her glass items. She'd ended up bleeding and almost losing the baby. The doctor couldn't say for sure if stress or the jarring from the fall had caused the bleeding. She was only two weeks off bed rest now. SShe'd been on bedrest for a few days and had had no problems in the two weeks since. She didn't need Mike returning and causing problems. And she didn't want to be afraid whenever she went out.

The sound of the doorbell jarred her and she jumped. God, not again. She rose and tiptoed to the peephole and looked out.

Scott.

Thank God. She didn't stop to think, just unhooked the chain she'd installed after Mike had moved out and let Scott inside.

*   *   *

After his sister had ripped into him, Scott had actually felt bad, wondering if he'd pushed Meg into something she wasn't ready for. He decided to call her … but his car just happened to pull off her exit. Yeah. He'd keep telling himself that.

He rang her doorbell, not even knowing if she was home. The door swung open wide, and he found himself facing a pale, wide-eyed Meg.

His protective instincts swung into high gear. "What's wrong?" He stepped inside and shut the door behind him.

"I… My ex was here," she said, her big brown eyes damp.

Rage at the thought of anyone scaring her, hurting her, filled him. "Here? As in inside?"

She shook her head. "No. I didn't open the door."

He breathed out a relieved breath. "Good girl."

"But he kept banging and yelling, cursing, saying we needed to talk."

"Not happening," Scott said through clenched teeth.

"Not if I have anything to say about it," she agreed. "I didn't answer him. But he's not going to just go away. Restraining order or not."

Her hands shook, and he clasped both his palms around her cold extremities and held on. Despite the serious situation, he couldn't help but notice how soft her skin was, how delicate she felt beneath his fingers.

"I don't understand. I don't want anything from him. Not a dime, even though his family can more than afford it. I just want him to sign away his parental rights. Why won't he just do that?" she asked, her voice trembling.

Scott filed the information about his family's money away for later. "People have strange reasons for doing things." He'd have to figure out Mike's. But right now, Meg was his only concern, and she needed to calm down.

He led her to the couch, where she'd obviously been sitting with her open laptop and notepad. He sat down, pulled her onto his lap, and she immediately curled into him, seeking comfort he was only too happy to give.

"It'll be fine," he assured her, wrapping his arms around her smaller frame. She felt so delicate, so perfect in his arms.

"I hope so." She curled her fingers into his shirt and rested her head against his chest with a small quivering sigh.

"I won't let him hurt you." He stroked the back of her hair, inhaling the fragrant scent of her shampoo. Memories of sliding into her wet heat hit him without warning, and his body responded.

He swallowed a curse, reminding himself she sought reassurance, not sex, but his stiff cock wasn't listening. It didn't help when she wriggled deeper into him, her face tucked against his neck, her breath hot on his skin.

He needed to think with his head. The one with common sense that knew she was frightened. "Hey." He brushed her hair out of her face. "You're safe now."

"I know. I just feel so stupid, thinking a piece of paper would keep him away. And I don't know what to do now."

"Well, first thing, let's get this visit documented by the police. You want everything on record." In case something else happened, which Scott wouldn't say to her out loud. For one thing, he didn't want to frighten her further. And for another, he wouldn't let that bastard near her.

She eased back to meet his gaze. "I can't prove Mike was here."

"I'll talk to your neighbors. See if anyone heard him yelling or recognized his voice. Okay?"

She remained silent, not looking at him. Clearly he wasn't helping. "What's wrong?"

"Everything." She pushed off him, sliding into her own space on the sofa.

He immediately missed the warmth and heat of her body, but she obviously needed distance. "Tell me."

She blinked her thick lashes. "I promised myself I'd stand on my own, and at the first sign of a crisis, I curled up in your lap and let you take over. How's that for falling back into old patterns?" she said, frustration and annoyance in her tone.

"Listen to me." Needing to touch her, to maintain the contact they'd been sharing, he placed a hand beneath her chin and tilted her head.

She met his gaze with wide brown eyes, and he was struck with a connection, a sense of *knowing* he'd felt from the first time they'd met. This woman tied him up in knots, made him want to fix things so he could see her smile and light up just for him.

Shit. He shook his head, not understanding how the hell he'd gone from *never again* to invested so quickly.

"What is it?" she asked, breaking into his too-serious thoughts.

He swallowed hard. Forced himself to concentrate on the thread of their conversation and not his emotions. "There is a huge difference between accepting help from a friend who is experienced in these things and falling back into bad patterns," he explained.

"Do you trust me?" he asked.

She nodded slowly. "I realize I barely know you, my judgment sucks, but that said, yes, I do."

The notion was humbling. "Good. So go make yourself a cup of tea or get some water. I'll talk to the neighbors and be right back."

"I wish I could do something useful," she muttered, but she rose and walked into the kitchen.

He couldn't tear his gaze from the sexy sway of her hips or the way her hair swung against her back. He bit the inside of his cheek and spent the next few minutes getting his dick to calm down so he could to talk to her neighbors.

His canvass of the two next-door apartments yielded only one result, but at least it was a good one. A middle-aged woman had heard the whole thing. And, she informed Scott, she was the same person who'd found Meg's phone and called her friend after

Meg had ended up in the hospital because of her ex the last time. Scott told her the police would be by to interview her and returned to Meg's to find her sitting at the kitchen table with a glass of juice in her hand.

"Good news. Mrs. Booth heard Mike, and she recognized his voice. I put a call into the station and asked them to send someone to take her statement. And yours."

She blew out a long breath and stared at her glass. "Thank you."

He didn't like seeing her so down. He eased into the chair beside her and tucked a strand of hair behind her ear, just so he could touch her again.

Her cheeks flushed, and a flicker of awareness lit her gaze. *There she was.* The passionate woman he knew had returned. "So what were you doing before Mike showed up?" he asked, changing the subject while they waited for the cops.

"Online shopping. Browsing, really. Making lists of what I need for the baby, comparing costs on the big items. Things like that."

"Sounds fun."

A smile lifted her lips, and damned if his gaze didn't zero in on that sweet mouth. The desire to kiss her sucker-punched him, but he remained in his chair, one hand clenched in frustration.

"It is. I don't know the baby's sex, but it's been fun

to look at all the cute little baby clothes and think about how I want to decorate for him. Or her."

"Is this a two-bedroom?" he asked, before he said screw it, threw her over his shoulder, and hauled her back to bed, to hell with any damned statements.

All he wanted to do was bury himself inside her while making her come hard and often. Then spend the rest of the night curled around her, keeping her safe and protected.

"No, just one bedroom," she said, oblivious to his sexual frustration and X-rated thoughts.

How the hell he maintained a thread of normal conversation was beyond him.

"I'll put the crib in my room for now. The bedroom is big enough."

He thought about his large house, the one he'd bought as a surprise for his soon-to-be growing family *before* he'd discovered his wife had had an abortion without asking him. But he'd loved the house, and moved in anyway. Four bedrooms, three and a half baths, plenty big for… Shit.

He was not going there.

"And since my room décor is neutral, I can do whatever I want in the baby area…" Meg trailed off, realizing she was rambling, and a hot flush rushed to her cheeks. "I'm really sorry. You can't possibly be interested in decorating talk." She could barely meet his gaze.

"Meg?"

"Yes?" She glanced up at the sound of her name, a rumbling caress coming from his sexy mouth.

His navy eyes were focused on her, and she felt his gaze as if he were physically stroking her skin. Goose bumps lifted on her bare arms.

"Take my word for it. If you're speaking, I'm interested."

And that interest showed in his intent stare and focus. Not to mention, she'd felt his erection pressing against her when she'd sat on his lap earlier. She'd done her best not to squirm in her seat.

"Look, I'm sure this can't be easy for you, but life has a way of throwing you curveballs. The important thing is how you roll with them. Have you eaten?" he asked, surprising her with the subject change.

"I was going to make myself a sandwich when I got hungry."

Her stomach chose that moment to grumble, loudly. God, could things get any more embarrassing? She had a hot guy she wanted to jump in her living room, and she was going on about baby furniture while her stomach made unattractive noises.

She'd just have to roll with it, as he'd said. "If you're hungry, I could make you one too? Unless you didn't plan on staying…"

"What's wrong?"

"I just realized… Why are you here? Don't get me wrong, I'm glad you showed up when you did, but … why?" She'd been so thrown by Mike, so relieved to see Scott on the other side of the door, she hadn't thought to ask.

"I came to see how you were doing. And—" He slipped a hand behind her neck, his touch a hot brand on her skin. "I didn't like not speaking to you all week."

Her stomach flipped delightfully at the admission. "I felt the same way," she said, unable to not tell him the truth.

"Now that's good to hear." He spoke in a low, husky voice. Then he moved in, his lips *this* close to hers, his breath warm against her mouth. "Because staying away was fucking hard."

His thumb swiped over her lower lip. A hot, aching feeling settled between her thighs along with dampness and a deep yearning for fulfillment. "Scott—" She didn't know what she wanted to say, just that she wanted, no, needed him.

His eyes darkened with serious intent. She wanted his hot mouth on hers desperately, and barely breathing, she waited for what he'd do next.

But the doorbell rang, jarring them both. She jumped, he swore, and the moment was broken.

"That'll be a cop to take your statement." Scott shot her a look of regret before he rose. He paused and drew a long breath.

His hands, she noted, were clenched in tight fists. At least she wasn't the only one frustrated.

He strode across the room to answer the door, giving Meg a chance to breathe. Stunned, she leaned back against the couch. What the hell had just happened? One minute they'd been talking about restraining orders and baby furniture and the next she'd thought he was going to fuck her right here.

Jesus. She rubbed her eyes and groaned before glancing over to where Scott spoke to a very young-looking uniformed officer.

She studied Scott, pleasure suffusing her as she took him in. In his faded jeans that molded to his hard thighs and taut ass, and navy tee shirt, he was *hot*. Well built, dark hair, and much more clean-cut-looking than the type of guy she usually went for. But everything about Scott was different, from his looks to his commanding air. Meg had been bossed around by men before, but Scott's brand of control made her feel safe and cared for, not put down and concerned.

He affected her emotionally and sexually, tying her in knots of confusion and need. For the last week, thoughts of him had distracted her during the day. She'd sit in her classroom and recall his big hands on her breasts, his mouth on her nipples, and then she'd hear someone shout … and she'd come back to herself, realize she was sitting alone, tingling and aware.

And the nights? He'd consumed her dreams, turning them hot and erotic. She'd actually feel his thick cock pounding into her, going so far as to cause her to orgasm in her sleep. She groaned and squeezed her thighs tightly together, aware and aroused even now.

But because she hadn't been able to stop thinking about him, his silence for the last week had left her thinking she was distinctly forgettable. Meg didn't sleep around often or randomly. That she'd had sex with Scott meant something, no matter how hard she fought the notion. She'd wanted to be memorable in return. Now he was here…

"Meg? Ready to talk to Officer Jenkins about what happened with Mike?" Scott called over to her.

At the mention of her ex, all hot, sexy thoughts vanished. She spent the next thirty minutes recounting her visit from her ex, providing a copy of the restraining order, and listening as the cop spoke to her neighbor. By the time the woman finished, Meg was surprised she hadn't complained to the landlord about the problems and noise Meg's issues had caused. But Mrs. Booth seemed sympathetic and understanding. She promised to keep an eye and ear out for her ex while Meg was at work.

Meg thanked her.

The officer jotted down some notes, then flipped the pad closed. "Okay, got it."

"You'll pay Mike Ashton a visit?" Scott asked, although from his tone, it came out as more of a demand.

"We're busy tonight," Officer Jenkins explained, though he didn't sound too upset about it. "And since nothing really happened here other than some noise and disturbance, I'll file the report, and it'll be on record. Meanwhile, keep your door locked."

Scott shook his head and muttered a curse as Meg walked the officer out and locked up behind him.

"He's new and not on my shift." Clearly agitated, he raked his fingers through his hair. "Don't worry, I'll have a talk with your asshole ex and remind him what the fuck a restraining order means."

"No, please don't." The thought of Scott confronting Mike turned her stomach. "It's fine. You don't need to get involved. The officer said if he bothered me again, they'd talk to him. I don't want to get you in any trouble with your superiors."

"Baby?"

She blinked, shocked at how *that* word, the one he used when he was in seduction mode, affected her. Suddenly her body burned hot, desire pulsing inside her again.

"Yes?" she managed to ask, her mouth dry.

"Don't kid yourself," he murmured huskily. "I'm already involved."

Oh. *Oh.* She swiped her tongue across her lips, and his hot gaze followed the gesture. "I… Umm…"

He grinned at how flustered she'd gotten. "Now I don't know about you, but I'm *starving*," he said in a tone that indicated the word could have two very different meanings.

She shivered, her nipples hardening at the various possibilities.

His gaze fell to the two points sticking out from her shirt, and a low growl sounded from inside his chest. "We'll get to that later," he promised, and her sex clenched at the possibility. "I don't expect you to cook for me, so let's go out and get something to eat. I want to make sure you have strength for later."

And this time she knew exactly what he was referring to, and she was in complete agreement. She couldn't resist this man and was finished trying. He'd see her get big, and the reality of a baby would send him running soon enough. She pushed that sobering thought away.

He obviously wouldn't let her get away with anything less than a full meal. "I like to cook. Think of it as my way of thanking you for showing up when you did." If not for Scott, she wouldn't have thought to call the police in once Mike had left on his own.

"You don't need to thank me, but if you're sure, I'd love to have you *cook* for me." He said the word cook in a rumbling tone.

So hot and gravelly was his voice, he might as well have said, *I'd love you to* fuck *me*. She didn't know how she'd make it through the next hour of cooking, dinner, and anticipation.

She turned away, needing to focus on dinner. "I hope you like grilled cheese. I have bakery bread and some really delicious kinds of cheese."

"I'll *eat* anything."

She shivered. God, everything he said made her think of sex.

But he kept her company in the kitchen while she pulled out her frying pan, cover, and other ingredients, and eventually she calmed down while preparing dinner. She was surprised to find herself comfortable with Scott in her personal space. Although … comfortable might not be the right word considering how intently he watched her.

And how, beneath his heated gaze, her body buzzed in all the right places. Places she'd been reminding all week to get used to nonuse for the foreseeable future.

Soon the sandwiches began to sizzle. A quick

check told her they were ready, and the delicious smell permeated the small kitchen. She served and was beyond pleased when he bit into the sandwich and moaned out loud, the sound too seductive to her ears considering where her thoughts had been.

"This is so good. Where'd you learn to cook? Because I gotta tell you, the most my sisters can manage is to slap cheese on bread in the toaster oven."

She laughed at that. "Well, my mother was similar. I took over meals at a really young age."

"Where was your father?"

She shrugged. "I don't remember him. He left us when I was four. And then it was just me and my mom. She didn't like being alone, and there was a revolving door of men after that."

"That sucks."

She nodded. "I couldn't agree more."

"I wonder what's worse. Not having a father or having one who preferred his other family." He paused, sandwich halfway to his mouth. "I didn't mean to say that out loud."

She reached out and touched his arm, too aware of the muscles beneath her fingers and his hair-roughened skin. "I'm glad you did. It's easier to share if you're not alone when you're doing it."

She'd come late to knowing the Dare family, having just met Olivia through Dylan a few months ago.

But of course she'd heard of Robert Dare, hotel mogul, with two families... There'd been stories. Whispers around Miami. But she'd never thought about how that had affected his kids.

"What happened?" she asked.

"He wasn't around, and I grew up thinking he was a father who worked really hard for his family. That's what he'd tell us, that he had business trips and he had to visit his various hotels. He'd come home for short periods, spoil us with gifts, and take off again."

Meg watched his face, noting the hard lines visible now. This wasn't an easy subject, yet he was opening up to her. "That's really rough," she murmured.

"It was. And it wasn't. My mom is amazing. You'd really like her—and she'd like you," he said, as if thinking about it had been a revelation. He smiled. "And I had my brothers and sisters. We were cool. But then one day, Dad came home, and there was a big *discussion*." He frowned at the word. "I heard Mom crying, and then they told us we had to go the hospital for tests. Christ."

He wiped a hand over his eyes, and her heart clenched at his visible pain. "They said that Dad had another kid who was sick with cancer and needed bone marrow. He wanted all of us to get tested."

"Oh my God."

"Yeah, except that wasn't the worst part. That

came at the hospital when we met his *four* other kids. And that's when the illusion of Dad working hard for his family blew up in all of our faces." Scott rose and took his plate with him to the sink.

She followed, placing her dish on the counter. "What happened to his sick child?"

"My sister Avery was a match. She donated bone marrow, and Sienna's healthy now. Thank God. But I hate him," Scott said tightly, the raw anguish in his eyes as stark as his voice. "For what he did to my mother, to us. For the lies. I don't hate them though. The others."

"That's because they didn't do anything except be born, and you understood that." Although it couldn't have been easy, and she admired the man he'd become, one who was compassionate and understanding despite the curveball life had thrown at *him*.

"Ian took forever to come around and accept the others," he said of his oldest brother.

"Not everyone handles things the same way."

Scott stood at the sink, head dipped, shoulders tight, arms braced on the counter. It was obvious he didn't repeat this story often and he hated the telling. Yet he'd opened up for her. She wanted to ease his pain. To take him in her arms and soothe him, the way he'd done for her.

On impulse, she stepped behind him and wrapped

her arms around his waist, resting her head against his back. "I'm sorry."

He accepted the gesture with a low groan. Then, taking her off guard, he spun around, and she found their positions reversed, her back against the counter, his arms bracketing her body, closing her in. He cornered her with his big frame, and her heart rate picked up speed, the serious conversation at odds with the heat passing back and forth between them.

"But you like your other ... siblings?" she asked, managing to hang on to the thread of conversation although his heat and delicious scent were distracting her. Consuming her.

His lips turned up. "Yeah. They're okay."

She shook her head and laughed. "You're a good guy, Scott Dare."

His smile slipped, and that sexy mouth turned downward in a frown. "That presents a problem then."

She wrinkled her nose, confused. "Why?"

"Because rumor has it you're attracted to bad boys." He braced his hands on her hips, lifted her up, and placed her on the counter, sliding his big body between her legs.

A low hum of anticipation took up residence in her belly—and other places.

"And I want you attracted to only me."

"Not much of a problem there," Meg said, her sex-starved gaze meeting his. "Even after promising myself I'm not going to get involved with any man, I can't stop wanting you."

Chapter Four

"Well, I want you too, baby." Relief and blinding arousal assaulted Scott at the same time. The wanting was mutual.

Talking about his family always got him wired, and his discussion with Meg had been no different, except now he had a willing, gorgeous woman he could lose himself in. And she gazed up at him expectantly, waiting for his next move. She needed release from her own rioting emotions too, and he was only too happy to provide it.

"Wrap your legs around my waist," he instructed her.

She did as told, and he lifted her into his arms and headed back to the bedroom. His pulse pounded hard, increasing with each step. Once inside, he placed her on the bed. From the minute he'd seen her wide-eyed and panicked earlier, he'd felt a primal need to protect.

And when she'd turned to him for comfort, he'd wanted to own her and make sure nobody could hurt her again.

He kicked off his sneakers, removed his socks, then reached down and pulled his shirt over his head, tossing it aside. "I don't know if I can take it slow," he warned her.

Her darkened eyes followed his every movement. "And I don't want you to. I told you once before, I'm not fragile."

She lifted her shirt and threw it the way his had gone, leaving her bare on top, no bra, revealing plump breasts, pink nipples taut and ripe, begging for his lips, his mouth. His teeth.

He hissed out a slow breath, unbuttoning his jeans and shucking them quickly. When he glanced back, she was shimmying out of her sweats, pulling her panties off along with them. She added them to the pile on the floor.

Then he glanced down and took her in—beautiful woman, all glowing skin and flushed cheeks.

"Look what you do to me." He took himself in hand and ran his palm up and down the painfully hard length.

"I am." She pushed herself backward and leaned against the headboard. Her legs were parted, giving him a good look at her glistening pussy. He groaned and pumped his shaft harder.

With an intoxicating smile, she crooked a finger his way. "Come here and let me take care of you."

He shook his head. Much as he wanted those gorgeous lips around his cock, he needed his mouth on her, needed to taste her.

"Not this time." He wrapped his hands around her ankles and pulled her toward the edge of the mattress.

"Aaah!" She shrieked in shock. As she realized his plan, she glanced up at him with dark eyes full of desire and need.

He grasped her thighs and pushed her legs apart, kneeling between them.

"Oh my God."

He chuckled, deliberately blowing warm breath on her soft, damp folds.

"Scott—"

He cut off her words with a long swipe of his tongue, and a shuddering moan escaped her throat, causing him to begin teasing her pussy in earnest. He licked her bare outer lips, working his way inward, sliding his tongue up and down, all over her sex, everywhere except the tight bud that needed his attention the most.

She bucked beneath him, writhing, groaning, cursing, and begging him to make her come. He enjoyed her like this, open to him, vocal, and willing to express what she needed. Because that was his mission, to satisfy her in every possible way.

But before he slid inside her tight, hot sex and found his own release—something that would happen way too fast once he felt her slick walls cushioning his cock—he wanted her mindless and crazy, so he kept up his sensual assault now.

He eased her down from the peak, turning his hard licks and nibbles to softer strokes, not wanting her to come just yet. He soothed her with soft flickers that didn't do anything except arouse and tease. Only when he was sure she'd lost that edge did he begin again, nuzzling her with his nose, inhaling her feminine scent, and sliding his tongue into her hot, wet channel.

Her hips began to buck beneath him, and he fucked her this way, tormenting her and again bringing her higher and higher with his mouth.

"God, Scott, please, I need to come." She arched and pushed herself up against his lips, her pleading voice so sweet to his ears, he was ready to give her what she needed.

He licked his way to her clit, easing up one side, then down the other. Her thighs trembled, and her entire body drew taut and poised. He flattened his tongue over the tiny bud at the same time he slid one long finger inside her.

"Yes, so close, so, so…" Her words were nearly

incoherent, and he hooked his finger forward, gliding the pad along her inner walls, hoping to hit just the right spot.

She screamed and shattered around his finger, her pussy contracting in deep, damp spasms, as she ground herself against him to ride out the assault.

Damn, but the sound of her coming, the feel of her suctioning his finger had his balls drawn up painfully tight. When he was certain she'd finished, he rubbed his mouth along her thigh, and she collapsed against the mattress.

He opened her drawer, found a condom, and sheathed himself in record time. He stood over her, hands on her thighs.

Heavy-lidded eyes looked up at him, a satisfied expression on her face that made him damn proud.

"You still with me, baby?"

Was she still with him? Barely, Meg thought, her body still spasming with delicious aftershocks. She managed a small nod, then took a second to study his too-handsome face, the sexy mouth that had just taken her to heaven, and the hard set of his jaw, so at odds with the caring man who'd been here for her earlier. She didn't know how she'd be up for anything, but she wanted to please him too.

He poised himself at her entrance. "You're so fucking amazing," he said, his words tugging at emotions she was having little success tamping down.

He slid into her slowly, letting her become accustomed to him, first the tip, then, inch by excruciatingly slow inch, the rest of his length. There was no need to take it easy. Her body opened for him, just as she feared her heart could do, easily and gladly, taking him inside. He aroused nerve endings she'd thought had passed out from his earlier onslaught.

Warmth spread through her veins, and a quickening began deep inside her, sending out delicious tingles to the rest of her system. He pulled out and thrust in on a slow, exquisite glide. She arched her back and tried to suck him in farther. He groaned and picked up rhythm, and so did her body, another orgasm shockingly not too far out of reach.

He leaned over and braced his arms on either side of her head, his gaze hot and steady on hers. "Feel me, baby?" he asked on a hard plunge that took him deep.

"Yes," she moaned, and he began to pound into her in earnest.

She arched against him, which had the effect of rubbing her clit against his hair-roughened skin. She whimpered, shocked by the needy sound, but it felt so good she couldn't breathe. She closed her eyes and focused on the sensations pummeling at her from inside and out. Lights and flashes sparkled behind her eyelids as another orgasm loomed closer.

"That's it, let it build," he said thickly. Every time their bodies crashed together, he ground his hips and pelvis harder against her sex.

Her entire body was on fire as he rocked into her, their joined bodies doing the work, taking her higher than she'd ever been before. The tremors didn't start small; they washed over her in a tidal wave of bliss. Nothing had ever felt so perfect or right.

He thrust a few more times, coming inside her as he shouted her name. He collapsed on top of her, and she accepted his weight, wrapping her arms around his sweat-dampened skin.

A little while later, they'd climbed beneath the covers. Scott lay propped up against the pillows, one well-muscled arm beneath his head. "You okay?" he asked.

She nodded. "More than okay."

Too okay, too sated, too happy for the situation she was in, but she wasn't going to dwell. Things would end on their own soon enough. She didn't have to do anything to push it along. She'd already learned she couldn't deny this man, nor did she want to.

"So … you really came here tonight because you missed me?" She lifted herself up on her side and met his gaze.

"I really did." His lips turned upward in a sexy grin.

"Good timing."

That ended his smile. "Yeah, about that. My brother runs a security company, and I'm going to have him start digging into your ex and his background. We'll figure out why the hell he won't just leave you alone without you having to talk to him again."

At the thought of having another conversation with Mike, she shivered, more out of dread that there would be very little talking done if he ever got near her.

"Hey." Scott pulled her against him, tucking her firmly beneath his arm and against his chest. His heat not only warmed her body but also took away the chill caused by fear.

"I can't afford to pay him," she said of Tyler.

"Yeah, well, here's the thing." As he spoke, Scott ran his hand up and down her bare arm, his touch arousing her despite the topic of conversation. Her nipples tightened, and she knew they were now poking into his skin. He kept up the light caress and continued talking. "Tyler offered me a job."

"Don't you already have a job? You're a cop."

"And I'm bored as shit. Not to mention, I'm on administrative leave," he muttered.

Oh, this was interesting. "Really? Why? What happened?"

He let out a low chuckle. "Apparently I don't follow the rules too well."

She shook her head. "You mean you'd rather make them? Who would have thunk it!" she teased.

Before she could blink, he flipped her onto her back and straddled her with his large body. "Are you making fun of me, Ms. Thompson?"

She wanted to laugh, but the stern look in his gaze had that giggle catching in the back of her throat. "No, I would never do that." She bit the inside of her cheek and tried not to let any sound escape. He looked like he was just itching for a chance to torment her if she did. She wasn't sure she could handle any of his sensual teasing.

He skimmed his fingers up the sides of her body, pausing as he came to the swells of her breasts and tracing beneath the sensitive mounds.

She stifled a long moan.

"As I was saying," he continued, "my brother offered me a job. Actually he wants me to buy into his company and partner with him," Scott said, sounding surprised. But as he spoke to her, he kept touching her, skimming her breasts with his knuckles, tracing a circle around her areolas with his fingers.

"Ooh." She let out a moan.

He narrowed his gaze. "We're talking," he reminded her.

She wanted to pout but knew better. For some reason, he wanted to mix up conversation and foreplay. Bad man. Somehow she had to focus, because she sensed this was an important topic to him. Very important, and he was choosing her to confide in.

She drew a deep breath to steady herself. "Why do you sound shocked that he'd ask you to be his partner?" she asked.

He paused, his hands stilling. "I'm impressed you picked up on that," he said. "Tyler's just two years older than me, but I always looked up to him. Especially after he joined the Army. He's successful now that he's home too. That he'd want me to join him means a lot."

She reached up and traced his jaw with her fingertips, the stubble prickling her skin in a delightful way. "You're smart and successful. Why wouldn't he want you?"

He shrugged. "It's just not something I ever thought was on his radar."

"Are you considering leaving the force?" she asked.

"Yes." He appeared startled at his admission. "I was considering it after he asked, and then I came here... You'd been traumatized and I realized, hell yes, this is what I would rather do. Protect people on my own terms."

She smiled up at him, pleased she'd been able to help him decide things, even if she hated what was going on in her own life at the moment. "I think you'll be fantastic at whatever you put your mind to."

He stared down at her, mouth parted as he studied her.

"That means a lot."

Her heart fluttered at his words, but before she could start dissecting his meaning, Scott grasped her wrists in his hands and pinned them back against the mattress.

"I need to fuck you," he said. "We can finish talking later."

She blinked up at him, her gaze settling on his darkening eyes, the razor stubble marking his jaw and his messed hair. Need and want poured through her at the sight of him poised over her. Wanting her.

"Umm ... okay?" Who was she to argue?

He tipped his head back and chuckled. "I can't remember the last time I laughed during sex. You're the whole package," he said as he settled his cock at her entrance, then swore. "Shit. Condom."

She bit her lip, wondering if she should do this. "Pregnancy isn't an issue, obviously." The words escaped, deciding for her. "And after my asshole ex got me pregnant and bailed, I got tested ... just in case. So unless you—"

"I'm clean. Tested for work. And I really want to feel you bare, baby." He raised his hips and drove forward, impaling her in one smooth thrust.

"Oh God." She felt him everywhere. So hard and thick, smooth yet not, it was an exquisite difference, and she reveled in the increased friction and sensation.

"I hear you." He slid out and back, his eyes a hazy dark blue, filled with desire as he picked up rhythm. No slow and easy this time, and she was grateful for it. She didn't want time to think or, even worse, feel.

He tightened his grip on her wrists and took her with unrelenting drives that had her coming without buildup or warning.

"Scott!" She screamed his name. Fought to free her hands, to grab on to him as she shattered, but he held on tight. The firm binding merely heightened the experience, intensified her orgasm, and she might even have blacked out for a second. She barely remembered him coming too.

Later, as he slept beside her, Meg's thoughts worked in a frenzied panic, as she tried to make sense of his sudden intrusion into her life. She'd been so determined to make a go of it alone. So sure she could easily hang on to her resolve not to get involved or rely on any man. Then Scott Dare bulldozed his way into her life and her bed.

She listened to his deep, even breathing and felt the heavy press of his arm curled around her waist. He was so strong and solid, so … reliable. He reminded her of Dylan, her high school boyfriend and, later in life, her best friend.

She blew out a deep breath. Dylan had been her one and only decent choice. A really great guy, and though their initial breakup had been mutual when they'd gone off to college, when they'd met up again later, she'd fallen again hard. He hadn't. And when he'd said they were better as just friends, she'd swallowed her feelings and pride and agreed, telling him she felt the same way. Better to have him in her life as a friend than to lose him because her feelings made him uncomfortable.

At this point, all she felt for Dylan was a brotherly friendship. But back then? His unwitting rejection had reinforced the truth. Good guys didn't find Meg worthy of sticking around. No guy did. First her father, who wasn't a good guy. Then Dylan, who really was. Point made. And she'd chosen accordingly after that, picking the worst, hoping for the best, and never, ever getting it.

Scott was a challenge because Meg knew herself. She had a horrible tendency to fall hard and fast, and this man, with his protective tendencies and bossy air, would make it way too easy.

But soon enough, he'd realize he didn't want to stick around as she grew big with another man's baby. Why would he want to raise someone else's kid?

A sharp pain sliced through her chest, but she relished the warning. The pain would help her remember and stay strong. Like Dylan, Scott would get tired of her needy ways. He'd turn away from Meg and the ready-made family she came with. No matter how nicely he handled it, if she wasn't prepared, his rejection would break her, like Dylan nearly had.

She'd just have to be aware and stronger than her heart. She would enjoy him now, but she wouldn't allow herself to get attached. Either she'd walk away first or she'd be prepared when he decided the time came.

*   *   *

Scott woke up in Meg's bed, the sun streaming through the windows, feeling one hundred percent different about this morning after than the last one. He'd pushed past her reserve and her walls, and with a little luck, she wouldn't grow cold and distant this morning. They had places to go and people to see. And he wanted to spend time with her outside of bed.

Last night had been phenomenal. Not just the sex, although Jesus… He'd never been with a woman without using a condom. Neither he nor Leah had wanted kids, and he'd always used protection. True, it had failed, but he'd used it. So Meg? Feeling her hot walls clasping around him, knowing there was nothing between them, it was heaven times a fucking thousand. Not to mention, she could read him well. She'd figured out immediately there was more to his feelings about Tyler's offer than just whether or not he should leave his job. The brother he admired and looked up to found him worthy of joining him as an equal. That also rocked.

Life was looking up, he thought, heading for the bathroom. He showered, once again using Meg's soap and shampoo, and getting hard as he inhaled the familiar scent. It reminded him of Meg, how she looked in bed, dark hair splayed around her, big brown eyes looking up at him with trust and arousal twinkling in the chocolate depths.

Fuck. He gripped his cock and began pumping with his hand, using the soap that smelled like her to lubricate his hand as he pretended it was her tight pussy tugging at him and milking him to completion. It didn't take long for him to come in long spurts, giving him a shot at getting through the day without dragging her into a secluded place somewhere to ease the constant ache.

He dressed in yesterday's clothes and decided a stop at his place was in order. He strode into the kitchen to find Meg standing at the counter, drinking the same pink protein shake as last time.

"Morning."

She turned toward him and grinned. "Morning to you too."

Muscles he hadn't realized he'd been clenching released at her easy greeting. He strode over, determined to set the tone for not just the day but for how he wanted things to be between them from now on.

He slid a hand behind her neck and pulled her in for a long, deep, strawberry-tasting kiss. He made sure to taste her completely, his tongue stroking the inner recesses of her mouth before he ended it with a quick swipe of her lower lip.

"Delicious," he murmured, meeting her gaze and amused by the dazed look in her pretty brown eyes.

"What's on your agenda today?" he asked.

"Nothing exciting," she said, turning away and heading for the sink, where she busied herself rinsing her glass.

He narrowed his gaze. "Remember what I said? Everything about you interests me. What's up today?" he asked again.

"I need to go maternity clothes shopping," she muttered, not turning around.

He walked over and surrounded her, wrapping his arms around her waist. "I can manage a stop by the mall."

She shook her head. "No. You do not want to come while I try on fat clothes."

She set the glass in the sink and attempted to wrench away from him, but he held her in place. "What the hell, Meg?" He turned her around and lifted her chin. Tears burned in her eyes, and he narrowed his gaze. "Fat clothes?" he asked, trying not to get angry and to understand instead.

She remained stubbornly silent.

He shook his head, totally at a loss. Sometimes women fucking confounded him. "What's with the embarrassment?"

"Men," she muttered. She sniffed and shook her head. "Sure, you're here now. My body is reasonably fit. I'm not stupid enough to think you'll still be here when I'm big like a whale, so can we skip the embarrassment of you seeing me shopping for stretchy pants with a pouch in front? I'm sure you have better things to do, and besides, I already have plans with my friend Lizzy."

He blew out a long breath, finally understanding. Or he thought he did. "I realize we're getting to know each other, but can you give me a little credit? It's not like I didn't know you were pregnant going into this." He was still attracted to her. And that was that.

"Whatever," Meg said.

He had sisters, which meant he knew she was going to believe what she wanted to, his words be damned. Fine. He'd just go along with the program.

"I need to stop home and change into clean clothes. Then I thought we'd go by my brother's and give him information to start digging into your ex. After that?" He'd concede defeat on this one. "You can go to the mall while I head over to work and talk to my boss."

"I wasn't aware I needed permission," she said, trying to remain sweet but make her point. She caught his *look*. "Are you giving notice?"

"Something like that," he muttered.

She wouldn't like the next part of his plan, so he intended to put off explaining it to her until her mood and feelings about him improved. He fully expected the fireworks to start again when she found out he wasn't leaving her alone to deal with her lurking ex.

*   *   *

The ride to Scott's took longer than Meg expected, and by the time he pulled off an exit on I-95, she had a throbbing headache. And when he turned onto a tree-lined street with set-back houses—big Spanish-style houses in the adobe coloring she loved, with gates around each—the dull ache turned to a searing pain. "You live *here?*"

"Sure do."

"On a cop's salary? Not that it's my business," she quickly said, realizing how rude and uncalled for her remark had been. "I'm sorry. I'm just surprised."

He turned, his gaze hidden behind really sexy aviators. "I get it. And for the record, I want you to feel like you can ask me anything." He turned into a long driveway and parked by a two-car garage. He pulled off the sunglasses and left them on the dashboard.

"Okay … then how do you live here?" she asked, feeling a bit braver but still overwhelmed by the upscale neighborhood.

"My mother's parents passed away, and when my grandfather died, he left us kids each a very nice trust fund. For me, it was a way to separate myself from my father's money."

She studied him without interrupting, wanting to understand this enigmatic, complicated man.

He shut the ignition and twisted to face her. "When I was married, we lived in an apartment in South Beach."

"Married?" This was the first she'd heard of it, and she couldn't believe the uncomfortable twisting in her belly. She had to remind herself that he'd said he *had been* married. He wasn't currently. And he'd been understanding of her past, so she could do no less for him.

He let out a groan. "It was a couple of years ago," he said, gripping the steering wheel hard. "And in truth, Leah, my ex-wife, was more interested in my family name and status than me. But at the time, I didn't really care. I thought I loved her, and I wanted her to be happy. What I didn't realize was that she hated me being a cop and thought I'd eventually give it up because she wanted me to." He shook his head. "I wouldn't, and we had many arguments over my hours and my job."

Meg let out a relieved breath. Because he'd only *thought* he'd loved his ex and because he was giving up being a cop *now* and his ex had nothing to do with why.

He reached out and toyed with a long strand of her hair. "What's going on in that beautiful head of yours?"

She glanced up at him and smiled. "That's a secret." And she wasn't about to reveal she'd been jealous.

His frown and the warning in his dark gaze promised retribution of the most sensual kind, and she squirmed in her seat.

"The house?" she reminded him.

"Right. Umm, things changed between us, and I decided we needed more space."

"Changed how?" Meg asked.

He grasped her hand and ran his thumb over the pulse point in her wrist. Her sex spasmed, and she swallowed a moan.

"I want to tell you," he said. "I just don't think this is the right time. Can you trust me and will you wait?"

She drew a deep breath. Now she was even more curious, but if he wanted time, she'd give it to him. "Okay. Yes. I can wait. Can I see the house though?"

His expression lightened and he nodded. "Let's go."

He opened the garage with a remote on his vehicle and came around to her side of the car, helping her out. He clasped her hand and led her through the garage. They walked directly into a laundry room that doubled as a mudroom, with hooks for jackets and a high-end washer and dryer along the far wall.

She still used the laundry room in her building, pumping money in to do her clothes, and this setup made her mouth water. Especially since she'd be trudging up and down with a baby in her arms … somehow, anyway. She preferred not to think about the details that were still seven months away and completely overwhelming.

They stepped into a white ceramic-tiled hallway, passed a powder room, and ended up in a massive great room that led to a backyard with a pool protected by gates surrounding the glistening water, and a gorgeous patio with padded furniture and a stone built-in grill.

"Scott, this is beautiful."

He strode up behind her and wrapped his arms around her, his body hot. "You really like it?"

What's not to like, she wondered. "I love it. Really."

She spun around, taking in the comfortable furniture, a deep maroon sectional L-shaped couch meant more for comfort than show, a huge table in front of it, and a recliner nearby. A fireplace with a large-screen TV sat in front of the sofa, and the décor was simple and tasteful.

"Did your ex decorate?" she asked.

He placed a soft kiss on her neck, causing her to shiver. "No. I didn't move in until after the divorce."

Her breath left her in a rush. That mattered, she realized, although she wasn't certain why.

"Someday we're going to christen this place," he said, his husky tone a promise that turned her body to liquid desire. "But not today, unfortunately. Make yourself comfortable; look around. I'll run up, change, and be right back."

She knew he'd showered at her place. His hair had been damp when he'd come into the kitchen. "Go ahead. I'm fine." He kissed her again and headed toward a staircase on the far side of the house.

She drew in a deep breath and took in this beautifully decorated, expensive home. More than ever, she was certain she needed to watch her heart. Because a man like Scott, who had everything going for him, was way out of her league.

Chapter Five

S cott returned from the bedroom with a small duffel bag in his hand to leave in his car. He didn't want to get stuck at Meg's place again without clean clothes, and he wasn't leaving her alone unless he was sure she was protected. He was just grateful she didn't ask about the bag because he doubted she'd appreciate the answer. Her independent streak would kick in, and he'd rather save the argument for another time.

When they arrived at Tyler's office, he took in the atmosphere as if for the first time, knowing his life was about to take a drastic turn. Double Down Security was located in a high-end building meant to impress big-name clients. Scott knew his brother didn't give a shit about appearances, but he did know how to play the game. He gave clients the perception they wanted and the protection they paid for. It was a win-win.

Scott had given his brother a heads-up that he'd be

bringing Meg by, and Tyler stepped out of his office to greet them. He slapped Scott on the back and turned to Meg. "I'm Tyler Dare," he said by way of introduction.

"Meg Thompson." She held out her hand, which Tyler engulfed in his larger one. "I can see the family resemblance," she said, her gaze going back and forth between them.

"Just a resemblance though. I'm the better-looking brother." Tyler winked.

Scott rolled his eyes. "Ignore him. He's a pain in the ass."

Meg laughed, the sound warming Scott inside.

"My little brother just can't handle the competition," Tyler said, his gaze never leaving Meg as he assessed her for the first time.

"Little, my ass," Scott muttered.

"And I hate to break it to you, but I don't see any competition," Meg replied, teasing Tyler right back.

A small smirk kicked up the corners of her mouth, and Scott burst out laughing. "She told you," he said to his brother, inwardly pleased she'd stood up for him.

Tyler chuckled. "I like her," he said to Scott. "Okay, so what can I do for you two?"

Scott turned to Meg. "I called Tyler earlier and explained the situation with Mike." He glanced at

Tyler. "I'd like to set Meg up with Luke. I want all the information I can get on her ex and his family. There has to be a reason a guy who doesn't want anything to do with a baby is still harassing her. She just wants him to sign away his rights. You'd think he'd be happy to do it."

Tyler's gaze darkened as he listened. Like Scott and Ian, the Dare men were protective of women. And once the woman meant something to one of them? Things got personal.

"Okay, I'll introduce you to Luke Williams. He'll open a case file and take information from you. Don't worry," he said to Meg. "We'll get to the bottom of things and get him off your back."

"Thank you," she said.

"Baby, are you comfortable talking to Luke alone? I need five minutes with my brother, and then I'll join you."

"Of course." Meg straightened her shoulders. "This is my problem. Take all the time you need."

"I think my brother considers it his problem too," Tyler said, wrapping an arm around Meg's shoulders and leading her toward the back rooms. "Meet me in my office," he called over his shoulder to Scott.

A few minutes later, Tyler rejoined Scott in his office. The space was large with a wall of windows overlooking the city. Because Tyler didn't have a woman in his life, their mother, Emma, had taken over decorating. The office proclaimed elegance and class, from the mahogany desk with intricate carvings and detail to the glass and brass accents and live plants, which Scott knew Tyler's assistant watered for him. In frames on the desk, there were pictures of Tyler and the family, their mother and their siblings. Beyond those touches, the office was professional.

"She's very different than your ex," Tyler said, cutting to the chase as usual. He didn't bother with small talk when he had a point to make.

"Yes, she is. I take it you think that's a good thing?"

"Rhetorical question." Tyler met his gaze with similar navy-violet eyes. "I don't like it that she's walking around looking over her shoulder."

"Me neither, obviously. I showed up last night, and she was freaked out. The bastard had been by, banging on her door, yelling and demanding to see her. The restraining order doesn't mean a damned thing to him."

Tyler rolled a pen between his palms. "Let's see what Luke comes up with."

"I made a decision," Scott said, also getting right to the point. He wanted to get back to Meg as soon as possible. "I accept your offer. I'm in."

Tyler rose to his feet and strode around the desk,

pulling Scott in for a brotherly hug. "That's fucking good news."

"Hope your military employee pals agree."

"No worries. You know most of them. These guys take orders like they were born to it. They know I've wanted to bring you in for a while now."

"Way to share that with me."

Tyler shrugged. "I needed you to be ready and willing to say yes."

Scott inclined his head, understanding. "I am. In fact, I'm heading over to the station after this."

"Giving notice?"

"If I were on active duty, yeah. Given how shitty things have been? My captain will be happy to have me gone." And Scott relished telling his boss he was leaving. "Besides, I need to free up my time to make sure that asshole doesn't get anywhere near Meg."

Tyler nodded approvingly. "She know you're about to be around twenty-four seven?"

"Not yet." Scott braced his hands on the chair and pushed himself up. "Let's go see what's going on."

Tyler eyed him through his assessing gaze. "You've got it bad."

Scott didn't deny it.

"Pretty damned fast."

He shrugged. "When you know, you know."

"And I wouldn't." Tyler shook his head and started for the door.

"Someday you will ... and I can't wait to watch you fall."

"Fuck you," his brother muttered.

Tyler chuckled and they headed to find Meg.

*   *   *

Meg liked Luke Williams. Blond, big, and imposing-looking, he was pure military, from his commanding posture to the crew cut of his hair. But he was warm and understanding when he listened to her story and wrote down the information on Mike and his family. Not that Meg knew much.

"When I met him, he was estranged from his parents. He said they were wealthy and demanding and expected more of him than he could possibly give." She shrugged. "I felt bad. He seemed like a nice, if misunderstood, guy."

It wasn't like she deliberately went after losers. It seemed like they became that way later on. Or, more likely, they didn't show her their true natures until after she'd been drawn in and had opened her heart ... and in Mike's case, her home to him as well. But she was finished putting up with shit from men. Done feeling used and taken advantage of.

"I just want to know what the hell he wants from me. Why he won't just sign away his rights and go away. I know my lawyer's sent the forms."

Luke looked up from the computer, where he'd been tapping away, taking notes. He spun his chair around and placed a comforting hand on her shoulder. "We'll get to the bottom of this. And we'll keep you safe."

She appreciated his words of assurance.

"Hey, Williams! Hands off the clients," Scott barked from the doorway.

Meg jumped at the unexpected angry tone in his voice.

Luke merely glanced up, met Scott's annoyed gaze, and grinned, slowly removing his hand, as if he had all the time in the world. "Nice to see you too, little Dare."

Meg stiffened, her eyes opening wider at the snarky, condescending comment. Was Luke looking for a fight? If so, from the furious expression on Scott's face, he wouldn't mind obliging him.

Jaw clenched, he started forward, but Tyler placed a firm hand on his brother's arm, stopping him. "Luke, Scott's agreed to join me here. Which makes him your boss."

Luke rose from his seat, strode toward the two men, and Meg held her breath. She wasn't thrilled with Scott staking a claim on her in front of his brother and Luke, yet at the same time, she couldn't deny a part of her liked his possessiveness. Rather, she liked the *thoughts* behind the possessiveness if not the behavior itself.

"You're joining us," Luke repeated. "That is great fucking news, man. Welcome aboard." Luke slapped Scott hard on the back.

The hit, which would have sent most other men reeling, didn't have an impact. Scott merely grinned and clasped the other man's hand in return.

"Thanks." Scott's voice deepened, the meaning in that one word clear. "And I meant what I said. Hands off *this* client."

Meg rose to her feet, determined to stop this ridiculous display. "Scott—"

"No worries," Luke said, both hands raised in the air in deferral. "I had no idea she was yours."

"I'm not anyone's!" she said. "And besides, do I look like a piece of meat for you two to fight over?"

Tyler burst out laughing. "I don't think you want either one of them to answer that," he said. "Have you made any progress?" he asked Luke.

Luke nodded. "She's given me enough to start."

"Great. I need to go meet with my captain. And Meg has plans with a friend."

"You two go on. We have everything under control and in place," Tyler assured him.

Meg hoped he was right. Because her security was at stake.

*   *   *

Meg didn't bring up Scott and Luke's pissing contest on the way back to her place to pick up her car. She didn't know what to do with the events of the morning, and she put aside thoughts of Scott, his beautiful home, and how she suddenly had a security firm she couldn't afford, digging into Mike's life. It was easier to focus on maternity clothes than the sudden one-eighty her life had taken.

When she checked her cell phone, Meg found Lizzy had left a message canceling their afternoon shopping trip because she'd come down with a nasty stomach bug. Determined to get this shopping excursion over with, Meg called Olivia. Luckily the other woman was up for a mall trip.

She had to admit she was surprised Scott had given in so easily on not accompanying her, but she was grateful. She needed a break from his intensity and protective nature. She liked it. Too much. So maybe it was her own surprising needs she needed a break from.

She parked and headed inside to the food court, where she'd agreed to meet up with Olivia. The other woman was waiting, but to Meg's surprise, she wasn't alone.

"Hi," Meg said, joining Olivia and a petite, dark-haired woman at a small table with three chairs.

"Hi!" Olivia rose and pulled her into a hug. "I brought my sister-in-law, Riley, along. Riley, meet Meg. I figured you and I could use an expert for our first maternity expedition."

Riley raised a hand and waved. "Hi, Meg. Hope you don't mind me intruding."

Meg shook her head. "Of course not. If you have advice, I'm happy to hear it. When my jeans wouldn't close the other night, I nearly burst into tears. They fit a few days ago. I'm a little overwhelmed," she admitted.

"I'm the mother of an eighteen-month-old. I now have expertise on things I never thought I could handle. Mind if I finish my coffee before we walk around?" Riley asked.

"Of course not."

"Want to get anything?" Olivia offered.

"No, I'm fine." Meg settled into a chair at the table, and the other women took their seats again.

"So speaking of your eighteen-month-old, where is your…" Meg trailed off, not knowing if Riley had a boy or a girl.

"Daughter," she supplied. "Her name is Rainey. She's with my mother-in-law." Like any good mom, Riley pulled out her phone and showed off a picture of her baby.

"Isn't she the cutest?" Olivia asked. "She has Ian's

eyes."

Meg leaned over the table and glanced at the screen on the phone. Actually, the baby had Scott's eyes, Meg realized, staring into the cherubic face with dark navy eyes and pudgy cheeks.

"She's absolutely gorgeous," Meg said, unable not to grin at the adorable baby with the cute smile.

"Thank you. She also has her father's … shall we say *dominant* personality? Stubborn as heck already," Riley said with affection in her tone.

"You don't say? That controlling personality runs in the family?" Meg met Olivia's gaze just as her friend burst out laughing.

"What am I missing?" Riley asked.

"Oh. Nothing," Meg said. "I just meant—"

"Meg is … involved with Scott," Olivia chimed in before Meg could formulate an explanation.

"Your *brother* Scott?" Riley asked.

Meg shook her head and swallowed a groan. "We're not really involved, we're just … I mean, Scott is helping me out with a situation." Meg liked her interpretation. Better than telling Riley she was sleeping with the other woman's brother-in-law.

"Is that how you want to play it?" Olivia asked, an amused smile touching her lips.

Meg blew out a long breath. Obviously nothing was sacred among these woman, and the truth was,

Meg needed female input. Especially from women who knew the Dare men firsthand. "Fine. We're involved. I think."

Olivia grinned, making it obvious to Meg that she approved.

"And I take it from your comment about my daughter's personality, you find Scott controlling?" Riley asked, laughter twinkling in her eyes.

"You could say that. But I'm not trying to insult him or your family," Meg rushed to add.

Riley shook her head. "Oh, honey. You think Scott's controlling? Ian is Scott on steroids. Times fifty."

Meg stared at the petite woman in awe. "How do you handle him?"

"Don't let her fool you. She has my brother wrapped around her finger." Olivia propped an arm on the table and waved her fingers in the air.

"Except it isn't always easy," Riley said. "And in the beginning, it nearly broke us apart more than once." She bit down on her lip. "I really had an issue with controlling men because of my past, and I wasn't used to turning to anyone for help. Especially when that help came in the form of being told what to do."

Like Meg had an issue with leaning on Scott. "I get that," she murmured. "I feel the same way. Scott took me over to Tyler's security firm this morning. I can't afford to hire them, but he has them helping me anyway." She shook her head. "I'm grateful but … I'd just promised myself I would stop relying on other people. Men in particular."

"But it's a different kind of reliance, isn't it?" Olivia asked.

Meg thought about the answer. "Yes. Very different. Before, I just wanted any man in my life, and I'd accept almost anyone to not be alone," she said, ducking her head in embarrassment. "Can we go shopping now? I don't think you two together women need to listen to my problems."

She rose from her seat and pushed her chair in so no one would trip. Olivia and Meg joined her, and together they walked toward the stores.

"I wasn't all that together when Ian and I met," Riley said, surprising Meg by continuing their talk.

She glanced at the pretty brunette.

"I fought everything Ian did for me to the point where I ended up in the hospital because I was so insistent on meeting up with my father and handling things alone." Riley placed a hand on Meg's arm, and they slowed to a stop. "My point is, we all have problems and issues, but please don't think you have to go through it alone."

To Meg's horror, tears filled her eyes at Riley's openness and generosity. She pulled a tissue from her bag and wiped her eyes. "Thank you," she said.

Olivia tapped her shoulder. "Do you think *I* had it together when Dylan and I started seeing each other?"

Meg shrugged. "I don't know. He didn't confide in me about you." Which had been her first clue that her best friend had fallen in love.

"Well, I was a mess. So wrapped up in my past I didn't want to trust any man. So listen to Riley. She's smart. And just know we've both been there."

"Except I'm pregnant," Meg said, pointing out the obvious. "And I honestly don't think your brother has dealt with what that means. So while I'm really grateful to have his support and help now, I don't expect him to stick around for too long."

She blew out a long breath, not wanting to dwell on that thought, or the tears would return, and they wouldn't be happy or grateful ones. "Now can we go shopping?"

"In a second." Olivia pursed her lips and hesitated before she spoke. "I also understand how you feel. And I'm not saying you shouldn't be wary. Be smart. Protect yourself if you feel you need to."

For some reason, hearing her friend say the things she'd already been telling herself about Scott really hurt. Because it validated her fears that he would eventually realize she came with too many burdens and he wouldn't stick around.

"Don't worry, I'll be careful. Besides, I have more to worry about than myself and my feelings." She patted her belly. "And I wouldn't burden Scott with my—"

"Whoa. That is not what I was saying," Olivia rushed to assure her, sounding horrified. "I just meant I think it's always smart to prepare for the worst. But Meg, it's okay to hope for the best too."

That's what she'd always done, with each new guy, only to be disappointed every time. But every instinct she had told her Scott was different. She knew for certain he desired her. In bed, they were explosive. She enjoyed talking to him, spending time with him. Getting to know more about what made him tick. And she had to admit it was a relief not dealing with Mike on her own.

"You need to start believing that things are going to turn around for you. And I think you should trust Scott. If nothing else, he's a man of his word. If he says he's in, he means it. If he changes his mind, he'll be honest about that too. But if he does, he'd be an idiot. And even though he drives me insane, my brother is not stupid," Olivia said.

Meg nodded. "You're right. I'm going to look at things differently." For right now, Scott wasn't going anywhere. And she should enjoy every minute for as long as she could.

"Now that that's settled, let's go buy out the store for you two pregnant women," Riley said.

With the heavy subjects out of the way, Meg had a blast shopping with Riley and Olivia. Riley did know what clothing was comfortable and what wasn't, directing them away from certain styles and brands and toward others. Meg and Olivia took turns trying on the padded bellies, making sure the clothes they bought would last longer than a few weeks. They laughed over what they'd look like down the road and ignored the more graphic things Riley tried to warn them about. Meg wasn't ready to purchase moisturizer for dry nipples quite yet.

From the store, they went for a late lunch. By the time they finished, Meg felt happier and more relaxed than she had in a long while.

She stretched her legs beneath the table. "This meal ... this whole shopping trip was amazing."

"I think we should make it weekly," Olivia said.

"My mother-in-law would love to have Rainey once a week. I'm in," Riley said. "I need girl time."

"Hey," Olivia said, leaning on the round table and speaking in what sounded like a conspiratorial whisper. "Do you think we should tell the waiter it's Rick's birthday? They make a whole big deal. All the waiters clap and sing, and everyone in the restaurant usually joins in."

"Who's Rick?" Meg and Riley asked at the same time.

"Rick Devlin. Your security guy." Olivia tipped her head to the right.

"What are you talking about? I don't have security." Meg followed the direction to see a guy with military bearing sitting at a table alone. Her stomach churned uneasily as realization dawned. "He looks exactly like the guys wandering around Tyler's office. But nobody said anything about someone *watching* me."

"Okay, I think I misspoke," Riley said. "Ian is Scott on steroids. Times twenty-five, not fifty. I think he's got more of that dominant gene in him than I realized." She sighed and took a long sip of her iced tea.

"Are you telling me Scott is having someone follow me?" Meg asked, horrified.

"I thought you knew!" Olivia muttered. "You said you were at Tyler's this morning and that Scott has them helping you."

"He's got a computer guy digging for information on my ex and his family!"

Olivia shifted uncomfortably in her chair. "When I recognized Rick, I just assumed you knew. He works personal security for Tyler. That makes him your bodyguard, for lack of a better word. He's had an eye on us all day."

"I'm going to kill Scott." Meg ripped a paper napkin apart in frustration.

"He obviously wants you safe. If you think about it, it's kind of sweet," Olivia said, obviously trying to dig her brother—and herself by extension—out of trouble. Because she'd called Meg's attention to the man.

"R-i-g-h-t," Meg said, drawing out the word. "Because if Dylan had a man assigned to guard you and follow you around without your permission, you'd find it sweet. Good to know."

Riley giggled out loud. "She's got you there," she told Olivia.

"Shut up," Olivia muttered. "I'm so screwed. Scott is going to kill me when he realizes I pointed Rick out to you."

"No, he won't. Because I'm going to kill him first. Besides, I would have figured it out sooner or later," Meg muttered.

Olivia blew out a defeated breath. "Well, if I'm going to get in trouble, and I will, I might as well go all the way. What I was going to say when I started all this was, I can't think of a better way to end the day than embarrassing one military man with a stick up his ass. Let's wish him a happy birthday."

Meg grinned and called for the waiter. Olivia was

right. Watching her bodyguard turn bright red with embarrassment and glare at them over his big hot fudge brownie sundae with a candle was the perfect way to end the day.

*   *   *

Scott was on his way to Meg's apartment, a large bottle of Perrier in hand, to celebrate his new job. He couldn't bring champagne to a pregnant woman, so he'd opted for something else that was bubbly. He figured he'd get there around the same time she returned from shopping, and they could *celebrate*.

His cell rang while he was driving. The dashboard indicated it was Rick, the guy Tyler had chosen for Meg's security.

He frowned. The more Scott thought about it—and he'd given his actions a lot of consideration as the day had worn on—the more he realized he needed to tell Meg she had a tail. On the off chance she realized someone was watching her, she'd assume it was her ex, and Scott didn't want to scare her. He also didn't like lying to her, even by omission. He should have been up front, and he would be now.

He hit the play button and used his speakerphone. "Talk to me," Scott said.

"Fucking women," Rick muttered.

Scott had known Rick for a while. The man had

served with Tyler during his stint in the Army, and they'd been friends ever since.

"What's wrong?" Scott asked.

"I was made. You didn't tell me your girl was meeting up with your sister."

Scott swore. "That's because I didn't know. I thought she was going with a friend." And Olivia knew Rick as well as Scott did.

"They treated me to a big-ass happy birthday sundae including singing waiters."

Scott shook his head, trying not to laugh at the women's antics because he was so fucking screwed. "Sorry, man. And thanks for the heads-up. I'm almost at her place. I'll deal with it."

"Want me to stick around?"

"No, wait for me to get there and then take a break. I'll call you if I leave tonight. You can cover me then."

Scott disconnected the call and shot a wry glance at his makeshift celebratory bottle. He'd hoped he'd be spending the night with Meg, but now he wasn't so sure he'd make it past the front door.

A few minutes later, Scott knocked warily.

Meg opened the door, a surprised expression on her face. Obviously she hadn't expected him, and that was fine. They hadn't made plans, but he was happy to see her. Hell, his entire body lit up at the sight of her pretty face and dark brown eyes.

"Before you lecture me, I looked through the security hole," she said, as if expecting him to reprimand her first thing.

"I figured." He held out the green bottle of sparkling water. "Care to celebrate my new job with me?" he asked.

She eyed the bottle, a pleased expression on her makeup-free face. "That's a considerate choice. Come on in."

He stepped inside, and she locked the door behind him. He couldn't gauge her mood, and that, more than anything, made him edgy. He wasn't sure whether or not to bring up the subject of Rick, then decided to take her lead.

He turned to face her. She definitely hadn't been expecting company. She wore a pair of pale blue silk shorts and a matching silk tank top, no bra. His gaze zeroed in on the pointy tips of her nipples poking through the light material, and desire swelled inside him. But he didn't kid himself that she'd be interested in fucking him, and he braced himself for the fight to come.

She took the bottle out of his hand and headed for the kitchen. He followed, watching her ass, the faintest hint of rounded skin showing beneath the edge of her shorts.

His mouth grew dry, and he could use a sip of that water.

She collected two glasses from the cabinet and opened the top. "So how did your boss take you leaving?"

"He wished me well. He knew how much I hated the rules… When I thought I could handle something, I resented having my hands tied by regulations." Scott shrugged. "He said I was better off being someone else's problem. I let him know I'd be my own boss, and we parted ways on somewhat good terms."

She finished pouring the drinks and handed him one. "To new beginnings." She touched his glass with hers, then, keeping her gaze trained on his, she took a sip.

He did the same, completely off-balance at her unexpected good mood. Actually, it was more than good. Her entire demeanor had shifted into a happy space, and he narrowed his gaze, unable to figure her out.

"Okay, dammit, why aren't you yelling at me?" he asked, unable to wait for her to slam him for placing Rick on her tail.

A sexy smile lifted her lips and she laughed. "Am I making you sweat?" she asked cheekily.

He liked this sassy Meg. "Yes. Care to explain?"

She lifted one delicate shoulder. "When I realized I

had someone following me—"

"You mean when Olivia pointed Rick out," Scott corrected.

Meg raised her hand. "In her defense, I had already mentioned we'd been to Tyler's and that he was helping me out. She assumed I knew about the bodyguard."

He inclined his head, less interested in his sister's role than Meg's feelings on the subject. "Go on."

"When I realized you had someone following me, I was furious."

Her eyes flashed with emotion and he braced himself. "Here it comes."

"No. Because as I drove home, I realized that, thanks to you, I could get out of my car and walk to my door without looking over my shoulder or fearing Mike would pop out of the bushes to attack me. And I realized how lucky I was to have someone in my life who wanted to look out for me." She took another sip of her drink and looked at him over the rim of the glass, a light blush covering her cheeks.

"So you aren't angry."

"I'm not happy you didn't talk to me first. Or warn me. But no, I'm not angry."

He stepped closer, drawn to this softer, more open Meg. "I'd already decided that I'd made a mistake. I would have filled you in tonight."

She ran her tongue over her lips, and his gut tightened as he followed the sexy movement. "Is that why you're here? To discuss security?" she asked.

He placed his drink on the kitchen counter. Took hers from her hand and set it down beside his. "No, I'm here because I can't stay away from you. But I'd much rather get the lecture out of the way so we can move on to more pleasurable things." He stroked his knuckles over her cheek, around her jaw, and down the soft skin on her neck.

She visibly swallowed hard. "Are you going to ask me before you make decisions that involve me from now on?"

"Yes. Unless you're not around, in which case I'll run them by you as soon as possible afterwards."

She nodded. "And if I don't agree, we'll reach a compromise?" she pressed on.

Now she was pushing him to make promises he couldn't keep. "I won't compromise on your safety, but we will talk." It was the best he could offer.

As he spoke, he trailed his fingertips along the loose edge of her tank top. Goose bumps prickled along her chest, her skin there flushed, and her nipples became harder peaks. He was dying to take one into his mouth, but they needed to finish up this conversation, and he shifted positions to accommodate his thickening length. The hard denim of his jeans was damned uncomfortable.

She let out a long sigh. Tipped her head, her hair trailing along the top of his hand. He actually fucking shivered at the soft tickle.

"I'll accept that for now," she finally agreed.

He narrowed his gaze. "Can I ask what's making you so … accommodating?"

And that was the change, he realized. She was suddenly more accepting of him in her life. More of a willing participant in wherever things between them might go.

"I spent the afternoon with someone who knows how to handle a domineering Dare man." And on that note, Meg wrapped her arms around his neck and settled her soft lips on his.

Chapter Six

On the way home from shopping, Meg had thought over everything Riley and Olivia said. Olivia, especially. Meg understood she could keep fighting this thing between herself and Scott or she could enjoy what he offered and move on when he was ready. Once she let go of her fear, it was surprisingly easy to let him in.

Especially when he showed up tonight with sparkling water and in an obvious panic because he'd been caught being high-handed. How could she resist the man when, beneath the control freak, he was so amazingly sweet? Not to mention drop-dead sexy. She'd looked through the security hole to find him on her doorstep wearing a pair of dark jeans that accentuated his hard thighs and a navy tee shirt that brought out the blue in his eyes and showed off the defined muscles in his forearms.

Making the first move was easier than she would

have thought, and she'd clearly taken him by surprise, which she had to admit, she liked doing. But the minute her mouth touched his, he groaned, cupped the back of her head in his big hand, and took over. He slid his tongue across her lips once, twice, then plundered. He kissed her over and over, long, drugging kisses that weakened her in the knees. He tugged at her hair, a gesture that she somehow felt in her core. He kissed her like he couldn't get enough.

She knew she couldn't. She wanted to feel his hot skin on hers. She grasped his shirt and pulled up at the hem, sliding her hands up his abdomen, feeling the hard muscles beneath her fingertips.

He broke the kiss and pulled in a ragged breath, giving Meg the opportunity to take over. She reached for the button on his jeans, popping it open and yanking down. He attempted to grasp her wrists and stop her, but she was faster, and she wriggled the denim over his lean hips. With a grunt of acceptance, he helped, and the denim pooled around his ankles. His cock sprang up before her, thick and hard, ready for anything.

She grinned and lowered herself to her knees. This wasn't an act she normally enjoyed, but something about Scott and how well he treated her made her want to give to him in return. And shockingly, the idea of going down on him made her mouth water and her sex ache with need.

"Damn, baby. Do you have any idea what it does to me to see you on your knees like that?"

She glanced up at him, suddenly shy. But if she had any reservations, they disappeared when she caught a glimpse of the heat in his gaze and the look of reverence in his expression as he gazed down at her. Leaning forward, she licked his erection gently at first, a long, teasing stroke of her tongue over his thickening shaft. He pulled her hair into one hand behind her and tugged hard.

The small hint of pain caused a surprising shock of arousal to spread from her scalp to her pussy. She moaned and grasped his erection in her hand. She eased her mouth around him, taking him as far as she could before sliding back the other direction. She wasn't an expert, didn't know what he liked, but she did recognize his growl as one of approval. And the hip thrust that pushed him deeper into her mouth definitely told her she was doing things right.

She slid her hand up and down, using the lubrication from her mouth to ease her way. Being Scott, he soon was driving the action, pumping into her mouth with long, fluid strokes. To her surprise, giving him pleasure provided her with even greater satisfaction than she'd ever imagined.

He grunted above her, his hand a steady presence

in her hair, every tug causing a wave of desire to wash over her. She moaned, the sound reverberating around him, and he thrust hard, the head of his cock hitting the back of her throat.

She fought not to gag and managed to breathe through, taking him even deeper.

"Damn, Meg, you feel so good."

So did he. She loved the taste of him, slightly musky, a little salty, and so very male. The idea of taking him all the way was a heady thing.

She worked him with her hand and mouth until suddenly he pulled himself out completely. "Not coming in your mouth, baby."

He stripped her out of her shorts and panties, leaving them in a pile on the living room floor. And wasn't that hot, she thought, as he picked her up and carried her to the bedroom with long, deliberate strides.

By the time he set her on the bed, she was panting with need.

"As much as I want to taste you," he said, positioning her on the center of the mattress, "I need to be inside you more."

He eased his hips back and pushed into her with ease. She was so wet and ready he filled her completely in one long thrust, hitting her sweet spot immediately.

She arched her back and moaned, feeling the

thickness of him everywhere, and her climb toward climax began almost instantly. She wondered if it was the hormones running through her body or whether it was being with Scott, but either way, she'd never been so sensitive or felt so much so quickly. And she wasn't talking just physically. Pushing those terrifying thoughts aside, she focused on the here and now, on the large man who owned her body when he was buried inside her.

"I love being inside you, baby." Scott groaned as she clasped him tighter in her hot body.

From the minute she'd wrapped her sweet mouth around his cock, Scott had needed more, and coming in her mouth hadn't been an option.

"Lift your legs," he instructed in a rough voice.

She complied, her long legs wrapping around his waist, and she pulled him farther into her heat. Using his upper body for leverage, he took a long glide out before plunging back in, hard and fast. Her slick walls gripped him tighter, her heels dug into his back, and he fucking felt her everywhere.

Sweat broke out on his forehead and back as desire and the primal need to own her washed over him. He took her hard, knowing she could handle it, understanding that she wanted him as much and as badly as he needed her.

They strove toward climax together, her nails digging into his back as she arched and ground against him. Physically, it was fast and furious, but at the core, there was something stronger pushing at him from his subconscious, an emotional connection he'd never experienced before, during or outside of sex. He knew what it was, even as he understood it was too soon, too fast. Even as it scared him.

And then her climax hit, and she screamed his name, shuddering around him, her sex clasping his cock in warmth and heat, and he came hard, emptying himself inside her and thankfully shutting down every other part of him, especially the emotions rampaging through his brain.

He became aware of her heavy breathing beneath him and rolled over, so as not to crush her.

She turned her head and met his gaze, a flush staining her cheeks. "That was … hot," she said, a grin on her face.

"That you are, baby."

She closed her eyes and obviously focused on slowing her breathing. "I don't, that is…" She stammered over her words. "It has to be the pregnancy hormones," she muttered finally.

He knew exactly what she was referring to. "It's not the hormones," he said, disgruntled. He'd had enough sex—he'd even had sex with his pregnant ex—to know better. Nothing he'd ever experienced came close to Scott and Meg together.

He reached for her, pulling her on top of him. "This," he said, punctuating the word by rolling his cock against her sex, "isn't just random fucking hormones."

Her eyes opened wide. She was surprised either by his harsh tone or his body's already thickening response. *That* sure as hell shocked him.

"I didn't mean—"

"Yeah, you did." He crushed his mouth against hers, plowing his tongue inside and claiming her in the most primitive way possible. When he pulled back, he pressed her head into his shoulder and closed his eyes, both startled and alarmed by his primitive response to her trying to brush off something he'd never ever felt before.

They lay in silence, her breasts crushed to his chest and her warm breath on his cheek.

"Scott?" She wriggled free, and he let her roll off him.

"Hmm?"

"This is really scary," she whispered.

His heart cracked a little bit at her admission.

"One minute I was pregnant and alone, dealing with a huge upcoming life change and an asshole ex, knowing I had to step up as the sole adult and take charge. And the next I have you barging in like some white knight, taking over."

He met her gaze, keeping one arm around her waist. "It's overwhelming for me too."

Surprise flickered in her dark eyes.

"But us—we're a good thing. You're not in this alone anymore." And he meant it. He was falling hard and fast for her, and he wasn't going to fight something that felt so right.

A tear fell, and he caught it with his fingertip. "Hey. What is it?"

She met his gaze. "I don't understand what you're doing with me," she said honestly. "And that's not putting myself down or even short-changing myself. It's a fact. But it's also a fact that I'm grateful you're here, and I'm not strong enough to turn you away."

"Good. Because you'd have a real fight on your hands. Some things are just meant to be."

"And in my experience, fairy tales don't come true."

He pressed a kiss to her forehead. "Don't think too hard, okay?" Lord knew he was trying not to.

She sniffed and nodded. "I'll try."

"Good. Are you tired?" he asked.

"Beyond."

"Then let's get some sleep."

*   *   *

Monday morning came way too fast. Scott stayed the weekend, and Meg couldn't remember the last time she'd enjoyed just hanging around and relaxing quite so much. He liked action movies and so did she, which meant they were able to agree on what to watch. They viewed *The Expendables* on Netflix, so he got his action, and she got her fill of Jason Statham, and moved on to the *Taken* series, which she'd missed in theaters. Liam Neeson certainly wasn't hard on the eyes either.

Before she left for work, Scott reminded her that Rick would be following her to school and waiting in the parking lot just in case her ex decided to make an appearance. Scott was heading over to his brother's so they could hammer out business details and talk to a lawyer to make his partnership and ownership of Double Down Security official.

He left her with a kiss and, "Have a good day, baby."

Her heart fluttered at that, and she set out for work. Maybe because her mood was good, the kids were on their best behavior and the morning flew by. When she sent them off to the music teacher for half an hour, she headed back to her classroom for a brief break but didn't get much time before the intercom sounded in her room. Allie asked her to come to the office, and Meg headed down the long hallway lined with children's artwork on various class bulletin boards before arriving at the office.

Allie's desk was directly in front of the doorway. "Hi," she said to her friend.

"Hi." Allie smiled but it didn't reach her eyes. "Meg, these people would like to speak with you." She gestured to an elegant blonde with a classic bob hairstyle and light makeup, wearing a dressy pants suit. By her side was a gentleman with graying hair and a well-fitting suit.

Meg didn't know them, and if they'd been the parents of her students, she would have. In a shocking change of pace, they'd all shown up for parent-teacher night. She didn't recognize either of these people.

"Ms. Thompson?" the man asked.

Meg nodded warily. "How can I help you?"

The woman stepped closer and spoke in a low tone. "I'm Lydia Ashton and this is my husband, Walter."

"Ashton? As in Mike Ashton?" Meg asked, as lights began to flicker in front of her eyes. She was suddenly dizzy. She reached for the wall behind her, seeking support.

The woman gave her a slight nod. "We're Mike's parents."

Meg drew a forced breath. She wasn't about to have a conversation with them here, where, heaven forbid, the principal could overhear. He was already upset with her pregnant single mother status. She had no desire for him to find her having personal meetings during school time.

Meg pulled herself up to her full height. "Let's go talk somewhere private. I only have another twenty minutes before my students return." She led them away from Allie's curious stare to a quiet part of the hallway where no classrooms were located. "Why are you here? What do you want?" Meg asked.

"Mike tells us you refuse to see him," his mother said.

Rick, her bodyguard, sat in his car, watching for Mike, who, thanks to online photos, he'd recognize on sight. Were his parents here because he couldn't show up himself?

Meg curled her hands into fists. "I have a restraining order against him, which means I don't *have* to see him. And he's already violated that order once. If the police catch him near me, they'll arrest him." Meg's legs shook, and she leaned against the wall to steady herself.

"Yes, that is unfortunate. My son is … a disappointment, to say the least."

Meg's eyes opened wide at that unexpected statement.

"That's why we're here. We"—the older woman pointed between herself and her husband—"want to know we'll be able to see our grandchild."

Meg shook her head in disbelief. "You do realize, when I told your son he was going to be a father, he questioned paternity," she said, still offended by his insinuation. "I'm happy to take any damned test. It's his. He was furious and he pushed me, hard. I fell and nearly lost the baby." She swallowed hard. "Your son is an abuser."

Her voice cracked, and she rested her hands on her stomach. "All I want is for Mike to sign away his parental rights. My lawyer sent him the papers, and based on his initial reaction, I don't understand why he hasn't done it already."

A terrifying thought occurred to her as she stared at the couple. "Has he changed his mind? Because I don't want him anywhere near me or my child."

A surprising look of regret and compassion passed over the other woman's face. "As I said, Mike is a disappointment. He isn't interested in being a father."

"Then why won't he sign the papers?" Meg asked.

Lydia Ashton turned, and a look passed between her and her husband, one Meg couldn't begin to decipher. "We don't know why Mike behaves the way he does," she said when she turned back to Meg. "He was always a trying child. He tested us at every turn, and when he found alcohol, we lost all semblance of control."

"You threw him out," Meg said, repeating what Mike had told her.

The other woman winced. "More than once, hoping he'd hit rock bottom and want help."

"But he kept finding unwitting people to see the best in him and take him in," Walter said, speaking up for the first time.

"Like me." Meg shook her head.

"Don't be hard on yourself. We know how charming he can be."

Meg swallowed hard. "Well, I'm sorry you drove over here for nothing. Mike knows what I want from him, and this is between him and my lawyer."

Lydia reached out a hand to touch Meg's shoulder, then reconsidered. "You do realize we're going to be this child's family."

"Not if your son signs those papers." Meg hung on to the slim hope that her ex would act on common sense. He didn't want anything to do with her or the baby.

"We don't want to lose access," Lydia warned her. "Family is very important to us."

And look what a wonderful job they'd done with their own son, Meg thought bitterly, but she wasn't cruel enough to say so.

Lydia shook her perfectly coiffed head. "We just want you to agree to let us see the baby, our *grandchild*.

If you do, perhaps we can persuade Mike to do as you asked and sign away his rights … not ours."

Meg narrowed her gaze. Would they really help her cut their son out? Or was this a game of some sort?

On the one hand, she understood where these people were coming from. She didn't have much in the way of family, and if her baby could have good, decent people in her life besides Meg… But that was the issue, wasn't it? She didn't know the Ashtons at all. Except for what Mike had told her about them being too controlling. And Mike's word wasn't to be trusted.

"We just want to be close to the baby. My hope is that you and I can work something out," Lydia said softly, her tone pleading. She reached into her purse and pulled out a piece of paper with a phone number on it. "Here. Please think about it."

Meg accepted the paper, knowing she'd do nothing *but* think.

Lydia studied her for a long moment, then inclined her head. "Thank you for seeing us."

If she'd had a choice, she wouldn't have, Meg thought. But then this woman had known the element of surprise would work in her favor.

Meg waited until she'd returned to her classroom to let her emotions free. Her shoulders dropped, and she fell into her chair, shaking. Although the Ashtons hadn't threatened her, they'd made it clear they wanted access to *her* baby. She covered her stomach protectively, wondering how she could gauge the truth about them.

Maybe Tyler's man would uncover information that would help her decide. Her own knowledge was limited. From her early days with Mike, she knew that controlling him via the purse strings was his parents' favorite sport. Although Meg had come to learn Mike did nothing to support himself financially, and so he relied on his parents, making himself subject to their whims. It was a messy family dynamic. Meg didn't want to be a pawn in their schemes. If there was a scheme. Maybe they were being honest.

Her head began to pound. She just didn't want her child to be drawn into an abusive or unstable environment. Meg had had enough of that herself, growing up.

Of course, after the Ashtons' visit, the rest of the day dragged on. Meg was preoccupied, so the whining and complaints of the children seemed exacerbated and more annoying. She kept a smile on her face and focused on the kids and her work, finally making it through to the release bell.

She always waited until her young children's parents came to get them. Today, two were late. She didn't want the kids to be scared or feel lost or unwanted. By the time Meg walked out of the building, most teachers had left for the day.

She exited and caught sight of Rick sitting in his car, watching. Just the sight of him made her feel safer.

She blew out a breath and was about to head for her own car when her cell rang. Hoping it was Scott, she answered without looking at the caller ID.

"Hello?"

"You stupid bitch! What are you doing talking to my parents?" Mike's scratchy yell caught her off guard.

At the sound of his voice, she dropped her bag. How did he know she'd seen his parents?

Oh God. He'd obviously been watching her somehow, and she swung around, searching for any sign of him in the few vehicles remaining in the parking lot, without luck.

She refocused on the call. "Mike! Just sign the papers, and I'll be out of your life!"

"I can't. If I do, my parents will cut me off for good."

Meg closed her eyes and groaned, things becoming clearer. This was about money. Wasn't everything in Mike's life? Hadn't he moved in with her when his parents had cut him off the last time?

Meg pressed the phone to her head, trying to think things through. She was already considering granting his parents their request, assuming they turned out to be decent people. Would that satisfy Mike? Would he sign away his rights and disappear from her life?

"What if I promised your parents *they* could see the baby? Without you," she made clear.

"No!" He hissed. "They'll try to take over its life."

"He or she!" Meg spat into the phone. "Don't call my child an it." Stupid, selfish bastard.

"What the fuck ever, Meg. Doesn't matter. They can't have a relationship with *him*," he sneered. "They'll make the baby their heir, and I'll lose everything."

Oh, boo hoo, she thought. How had she ever thought he was charming? He had been though. Before the alcohol. Or before he'd let her see this side of him, anyway.

"What do I have to do to get you out of my life?" she asked as she picked up the items that had fallen out of her open purse.

"What I told you to do from the beginning. Get rid of the fucking baby. I'll go back to being the perfect son, and my parents won't have another heir to threaten me with."

Horrified, she was just about ready to hit disconnect when Mike spoke again. "You do it or I'll do it for you."

Meg dropped her phone and forced a gulp of humid Florida air into her lungs. She remained on her knees, unable to believe what she'd just heard.

"Meg!" An unfamiliar male voice called her name. She swung her head around to see Rick coming toward her.

He knelt and tossed the remaining items on the floor into her purse, then helped her to her feet. "What happened?"

She looked into steady green eyes and drew a calming breath. "I had a visit from my ex's parents at school earlier today. And Mike called just now."

Rick swore. "Phone," he demanded, holding out his hand.

She pulled her cell from her bag, unlocked it, and handed it to him. He checked the last call and redialed.

"Probably a burner phone," he muttered. "Fuck. Let's go." He grasped her elbow and led her toward his car.

She dug in her heels. "Wait, my car."

"We'll get it back to you later."

"But—"

"Do you want to call Scott and tell him why you won't get in the car with me and let me keep you safe? Or would you rather I did it for you? Or you could do what I say." With the push of his thumb, he unlocked his black Ford.

She narrowed her gaze at him. "What is with you bossy men?" she asked as she let him open the passenger door.

"We get the job done," he muttered.

She pulled on her seat belt and leaned her head against the seat, exhaustion suddenly overwhelming her. When had her life become so complicated and *why*?

*   *   *

Scott spent the day familiarizing himself with his brother's place of business. Now his business as well. Or it would be once they made it official with paperwork.

He couldn't remember the last time he'd felt so right about a decision. Like he was finally in a place where he belonged. He could push boundaries and rules when necessary without someone coming down on him for violating department policy. He breathed out a slow breath, grateful that the guys here had welcomed him too. They'd given him shit for not being able to hack it on the force, slapped him on the back, and that was that.

Scott took over a small office across the way from Tyler, refusing any offer to exchange with someone for a larger one. He didn't need space or the status of a big room. He just needed to breathe, and he could do that here.

As for Meg's ex, he now had a file on the man and his family, and it appeared Mike was the black sheep son who they had unsuccessfully tried to place in rehab for alcohol abuse. He had also been adopted as a baby. And that was all he knew. For now. Luke was still digging. He groaned and looked out the window at his glorious view of the parking lot.

An incongruous dark sedan pulled into the lot and parked. Scott blinked against the glare of the sun as Rick climbed out, met Meg on her side, and escorted her toward the building, a hand beneath her arm. Tension radiated from the man who was assigned to look out for her, while she looked subdued and upset.

"Shit." He rose and headed to meet them out front, wondering what the hell had happened now.

Chapter Seven

"I want to go home," Scott heard Meg tell Rick as he met them in the front area.

Scott joined them by reception. "What happened?" He glanced at Meg, who, up close, was pale and completely disheveled, dust marks on her black leggings, her hair falling out of her clip in disarray. She was still beautiful.

"I'll let her tell you. I'll be getting a trace on that number," Rick said, striding away, Meg's cell phone in hand.

Scott narrowed his gaze. Needing answers, he grasped Meg's hand and pulled her into his office. By the time he closed the door behind him, his heart was pounding hard in his chest.

He turned to her, immediately cupping her face in his hands. "Are you okay?" he asked first.

She nodded. "I'm fine. A little shaken up but I'm okay. I told Rick to take me home so I could pull myself together, but he insisted on coming here."

"What happened?" he asked again. "From the beginning."

"I had a visit from Mike's parents. They came by school to talk to me about visitation with the baby. And believe it or not, that wasn't what has me rattled. Well, it does, but not in an *I'm scared* sort of way."

Scott tried to keep up with the flow of conversation and rambling. "Okay, we'll deal with the parents in a few minutes." He settled himself on his mostly empty desk and slid his arms around her, easing her down beside him. "What else went on?"

"I was leaving school for the day when my phone rang. It was Mike, and he knew I'd been with his parents, which means he's watching them. Or me. Or both. I don't know." She brushed her hair off her face with a shaking hand.

"Slow down. Tell me what he said."

Big brown eyes turned his way. "I told him to sign the papers and I'd be gone from his life. He said if he did, his parents would cut him off financially. I figured that was because they want to see the baby, like they told me. So I offered to give them that right—but not him."

He opened his mouth to ask what the hell she was thinking, but she held up a hand in front of him.

"I was just feeling out the situation for information, that's all. I wouldn't do something like that without more facts. Anyway, I figured he'd jump on the chance to give his parents what they wanted, right?"

"I'd think so, but I'm guessing not?"

She shook her head. "He said if I did that, they'd just make the baby their heir and he'd lose everything."

"So now we know it's about money." Scott clasped her hands in his, hating how cold and clammy they felt. He rubbed them between his palms in an attempt to warm her, succeeding in warming himself up too, in all the wrong ways.

"I asked him what I had to do to get him out of my life, and he said I should do what he told me from the beginning. Get rid of the baby—"

Those words triggered something primal and still raw inside Scott, and he let out a low, angry growl.

Meg's shocked gaze darted up, meeting his. "What's that all about?"

"He threatened you," Scott hedged, not wanting to reveal his personal shit here and now.

"But—"

"Later," he promised. "I will tell you everything when we get home later."

She nodded. "It's the second time you've put me off on something. I'm holding you to that promise," she said, her voice strong.

"Okay." He'd suck it up and explain about Leah and the baby. Later.

Her shoulders relaxed at his promise.

Right now, though, this was about Meg, and she wanted to keep her baby, unlike his ex, who'd aborted without his knowledge.

"Back to you. And Mike," Scott said.

A defiant expression crossed her pretty face. "If I wasn't going to get rid of the baby when I found out about it and was in shock, what makes him think I'll do it now?" She pulled her hands free, wrapping them around her stomach.

As a man who'd had everything ripped away from him suddenly and without warning by a selfish bitch who'd never given his feelings a thought, Scott eyed this protective woman with wonder and awe.

"Is that everything?" he asked gruffly.

She shook her head, her eyes damp. "He told me to get rid of it or he'd do it for me," she whispered.

Scott swore, possessive feelings rushing through him. "He won't get near you," he promised. He'd protect Meg and her unborn baby, but more than that, he'd make her feel safe. "I've got you."

She threw herself into his arms, wrapping herself around him and holding on tight. "I don't know why you're with me, but I'm so glad you are."

She fit against him, and he buried his face in her

hair, breathing in her sexy scent. "It'll be okay."

She eased back, glancing up. "I believe you." Her gaze intense, she lowered her head until her lips touched his, a soft press of her mouth, and he was lost. He skimmed his tongue back and forth over the seam of her lips, coaxing her open, sliding inside.

She welcomed him eagerly, the kiss going on, a long stroking tangle of tongues. He loved tasting her, could kiss her forever. Even with his cock begging to be freed, he could get lost in her mouth for hours. He lifted her shirt, gliding his knuckles up her sides and cupping her breasts through the lace bra.

"I may keep my desk empty just for this alone," he muttered before burying his mouth against her neck.

He suckled lightly, knowing she wouldn't be happy if he left a mark. His inner beast wanted to claim her that way, but he respected her too much to cause trouble for his hot, sexy kindergarten teacher.

She wriggled closer, and he pulled her astride him, her knees on either side of his thighs. His cock jumped in eagerness, but it wasn't getting any real action. She shifted, settling her sex over the hard swell of his erection, and as he rocked her against him, she curled her fingers around his shirt and moaned.

"I know what you need, baby. Let me take the edge off of your stress." He braced his hands on her hips and moved her back and forth, heeding her soft sighs and increasingly rapid breathing.

He gritted his teeth at the heated press of her mound against his confined cock, promising himself release later. This wasn't about him. Since he'd met Meg, nothing he did was about anyone or anything other than her.

"Oh, Scott. This feels so good." Her hips shifted restlessly, her lower body gyrating hard against him.

"Pretend I'm inside you. Hard. Big. Hot. Fucking you and giving you what you need."

She tipped her head back, which thrust her pelvis forward, and she let out a shuddering scream.

Somehow he silenced her, slamming his mouth down on hers, capturing the sound of her orgasm at the same time her body seized over and around his. As she rode out her release, the steady grind of their bodies nearly killed him. He held back somehow, trying to focus on counting in his head and not on the sexy-as-fuck woman coming apart in his arms.

She finally collapsed against him, and even he needed a minute or two to catch his breath. He wasn't sure how much time had passed when he heard the knock on his door.

Meg tried to push off him, but he held on. "Come in."

"Rick's guess was right. It was a burner," Tyler said as he stepped inside. His gaze locked on Scott's before glancing at the embarrassed female bundle in his arms. Tyler grinned. "Want me to come back later?"

"No, go on," Scott said.

Meg pinched his side hard.

He managed not to grunt in surprise.

Tyler leaned against the doorframe. "Like I said, dickhead called from a disposable. No trace. And Rick filled me in on the rest of what went down today. Your best bet is to try talking to the parents. See what influence they have on their kid."

Scott ran a hand over Meg's back, still very aware of the soft woman in his arms. "We'll figure it out," he said to his sibling.

Tyler nodded, grinned, and stepped out, shutting the door loudly behind him.

"Oh my God, that was mortifying!" Meg pushed off his lap and adjusted her clothing, smoothing wrinkles from her leggings and fixing her shirt, which was hanging askew. "I was straddling you, and we'd just, I'd just…"

Scott knew well what they'd just done. His dick still stood at alert, and his balls were probably blue. "Relax, it's my office. And Tyler doesn't care."

"Well, I do." She pulled her clip out and tried to fix her hair. "I need to go home and pull myself together. Relax. But I need my car, and that's at the school, so you can just take me there now."

She was so adorably flustered, and he hated to stress her out more, but it couldn't be helped. "Okay, first, yes, you need to go home. But not to shower and relax. I want you to pack up your things and come home with me."

"What?" she squeaked.

"Mike is following you. He's threatened you. Your apartment doesn't have security, you have no alarm, and it's not safe. I want you where I can keep an eye—and other body parts—on you," he said, trying to ease the whole dominant thing with a wink and a tease.

She narrowed her gaze. "I know what you're doing."

"I'd be disappointed if you didn't."

Meg blew out a long breath and paced back and forth in the small office. She might have just had an awesome orgasm, but her stress had returned the minute Tyler Dare had walked in on them. "I promised myself I'd think things through. When it came to dealing with you, to coping with Mike, I swore I'd be smart."

Smart as in not falling hard for this incredible man who was doing his utmost to protect her and keep her safe. Who was insinuating himself in her life and making himself welcome and needed. She shook her head in denial. Nobody was indispensible, and she would be fine on her own. But she also knew better than to put pride, ego, or past mistakes ahead of keeping her and the baby out of harm's way.

"Staying with you until this Mike situation is resolved is the smart, safe thing to do," she conceded, and not easily. To that end, and only that end, Scott's solution made sense. To everything but her heart.

Surprise etched his handsome face. "Thank you for making it easy."

"Thank you for offering your house." She turned away, not wanting to look into those dark navy eyes for too long. She could drown in them.

"I'll arrange to have your car brought there."

"Thank you," she said softly. "Can we go now?"

"Yes."

"Good." Because not only did she want to shower and rest, she wanted the answers Scott had promised her earlier. And she intended to get them.

*　　*　　*

Scott was grateful Meg needed to unwind when they returned to his house and she didn't insist on talking. Oh, he knew he'd have to come clean eventually, but he appreciated the time to grill steaks, have a beer, and listen to her humming to the music she played through her cell phone while she prepared a tossed salad. He liked the sounds of her moving around in his kitchen, making herself at home. Normalcy wasn't something he had much of, and being with Meg brought him a shocking kind of peace.

She'd taken a long shower first, and now she walked around his kitchen in one of those silky short outfits she preferred, this one in soft beige. The kind that showed everything and gave him a permanent hard-on. If he hadn't caught her wearing something similar when she'd believed she'd be alone, he'd have thought she was deliberately torturing him.

After dinner, they moved out to the patio, relaxing on adjacent lounge chairs. He stared out at the pool, enclosed by a fence for baby and child safety, remembering the time and effort he'd put into designing the yard after he'd bought the house. The yard had been a priority, and he'd started on the back immediately because suddenly he'd been looking forward to a whole different kind of life. Leah hadn't been.

He tilted his head and glanced at Meg. She studied him in silence, serious brown eyes taking him in. Waiting.

"I guess it's time," he said.

She lifted her shoulder, which had the bonus effect of raising her breasts beneath the flimsy top. Her nipples, tight from the slightly cooler night air, peaked against the sheer tank, and Scott bit back a groan. There was way too much to come for his mind or body to consider that kind of detour.

"Only if you want to. I'm not going to force you to bare your soul," she said. Her little tongue darted out, moistening her bottom lip, and he was tempted to say fuck it, straddle her on the recliner, and forget all about his past.

But she'd hold it against him if he didn't talk or tried to distract her. He got it. Her life was an open book for him. He'd made himself a part of hers. Fair was fair. No matter how much he hated revisiting that time in his past, he would.

He leaned his head back against the cushioned headrest but kept his gaze on hers. "You know about my family. My father never being home, finding out about his other kids and his mistress. I guess you could say it left a very sour taste in my mouth about marriage."

She lay on her side and curled her knees in, getting comfortable. "I guess a crappy childhood leads you to go one of two ways. You search for something better or you decide never again."

Meg wanted better. Scott knew that without asking. For all her talk about standing on her own—and he believed that's what she wanted—deep down inside, she also desired the happily ever after you only read about in books. Which begged the question: What was he doing getting so involved with her now? Any way he sliced it, she'd be having a baby and settling into a domesticity he'd never envisioned for himself before or after Leah.

"Go on," Meg said into his extended silence.

He blinked, her voice bringing him back to the present. He cleared his throat. "You're right. I had no intention of getting married."

"So what happened?"

He shrugged. "Hurricane Leah. I met her at a Thunder Christmas party. She was a model and had come with one of the players, but they weren't getting along and broke up before the night even ended. He left her there; she was stranded…"

"And you stepped up. Scott Dare, to the rescue." She waved her hand through the air.

He heard the bitter irony in her tone, but he couldn't deny it. Apparently he had a pattern, or at least he'd done the same thing twice. Seen a woman in trouble and stepped in to save her.

Instead of addressing Meg's comment, he merely went on. "We seemed to want the same thing out of life, which, back then, was a good time. And I liked having someone to come home to. We moved in together pretty quickly. I won't deny that I knew she liked the status of being with a Dare. She wanted the perks that came along with having my brother president of the Thunder and my father owning a string of luxury hotels. To be honest, it didn't bother me at the time." He glanced at Meg.

"That's almost as sad as me dating men, hoping they'd change, and keeping them around long past their expiration date so I wouldn't be alone," she said.

Wow. That hurt, he thought, letting her words bounce around his brain. But… "You have a point there. And if I'd had my brain in the right place, I might have realized it was inevitable that the relationship would go south. Instead, I listened to my—"

Meg laughed before he could finish the sentence. "I get the point."

"Right. But I really did think I loved her at the time. I knew she wanted to get married, what we had was fine, fun … so I agreed. And it remained fun until about a week after the honeymoon when she started pressuring me to leave the force and take a job with Ian or my father."

Meg's nose wrinkled in distaste. "First of all, you would never work for your father. I got that about you pretty quickly. And second, sitting behind a desk with nothing to stimulate you would kill you. You need the excitement of some kind of investigative work. Surveillance, digging into facts, reading motives, going after bad guys, and helping people." She shot him a look filled with pure disappointment. "I can't believe you married someone who didn't understand that about you."

Scott shook his head, a mixture of emotions filling him as he listened to Meg's succinct summary. In a couple of weeks, she knew him better than Leah, who he'd been with for a year before they'd married. Meg not only understood who he was, she innately knew what he needed. And holy shit, that blew him away.

"Okay, well, yes, you're right. I like to chalk it all up to me being young, horny, and stupid."

"Your words, not mine." She grinned, and the smile reached inside her, lighting up her eyes with a sparkling twinkle. "I think there's more though?"

He ran a hand through his hair. "Yeah, there's more. Leah and I had agreed neither one of us wanted children."

Meg's expression dimmed at that, and Scott felt the loss of that megawatt smile.

Might as well get it over with, he thought. "But then Leah got pregnant, and it was a shock because we'd both been careful."

"The unexpected does happen," Meg said dryly.

The sun began to set behind her, the fading rays hitting her hair, burnished auburn and red highlights capturing his attention.

He wished he were free to wrap himself up in her, but this story was having an impact on them both, and he felt her curling into herself. He hated it, but he had to finish and then deal with the fallout.

"It started as shock, but like you, I wrapped my head around the reality pretty quickly, and I started thinking about a life beyond just myself and Leah. And I could see it. The family I never thought I wanted, kids I didn't think I'd have... I got excited. And invested."

"You bought this house." Meg's gaze fell on the structure behind him.

He nodded. "But Leah wasn't as fired up as I was. In fact, she was depressed. I wanted to show her how good things could be. So yeah, I bought it as a surprise and started the renovations immediately. Eventually I brought her out here. I figured if she could look at things through my eyes, she'd see what I saw and want the same thing."

"Except she didn't?" Meg asked.

Scott shook his head, and Meg wondered what in the world was wrong with the woman Scott had married. Meg's baby's father had thrown her against the nearest wall when he'd found out she was pregnant. Scott had bought a fricking McMansion. And his ex-wife still hadn't been happy.

"What happened?" Meg asked, needing to hear the rest.

"She looked around, asked me why in the hell I'd think she wanted to live anywhere but South Beach, where the parties and the action was. At which point, she informed me she'd already had an abortion and had just been waiting for the right time to tell me."

Meg sucked in a shallow breath and nearly choked on her own saliva. "Oh my God."

"Yep. Didn't even ask me how I felt about it ahead of time. She didn't give me a choice. Hell, she didn't give my feelings any thought at all. And I'd already made it perfectly clear that, while I might be surprised, her pregnancy was a gift in disguise. I wanted that baby."

He pushed himself up and paced in front of Meg's chair, his agitation clear.

Meg's stomach suddenly hurt, and she eased back against the soft cushion and wrapped her arms around her knees. "That's awful."

He nodded. "It sucked."

"So you divorced her."

"Yep. Her behavior and selfish actions mocked my change of heart. I should have gone with my gut instinct after all. My father had taught me a hard-won lesson."

"What lesson was that?" Meg asked softly, almost afraid to hear.

He let out a harsh sound she couldn't interpret. "That the whole family thing is for suckers and happily ever after only happens in fairy tales."

Meg ducked her head, not wanting him to see how

much she hurt for him … and for herself. Because like Scott, she'd seen the worst in relationships, but unlike him, she kept wanting to believe in the fairy tale. Even now. And she obviously wouldn't be finding it with him.

Her eyes filled and she blinked back the tears. Despite having promised herself she wouldn't hold out any hope for something more with Scott, she knew now that she had. Having him around, so caring and invested in her safety, him looking at her like he wanted to eat her up and come back for seconds... A tiny kernel of hope had taken up residence in her heart. Thank God he'd revealed his past and his feelings about marriage and family now and not down the road when Meg would really have begun to delude herself into seeing what she wanted to see. After all, she was good at that.

"I'm really sorry," she whispered.

"At least now you know why I reacted the way I did when you told me Mike demanded you terminate the pregnancy." His tone softened, as it always did when he spoke to her. "I know how much you want this baby." He stood in front of her chair, so big, handsome, and at the moment, self-contained.

He'd pulled into himself much the way she had. And that was a good thing, she told herself. Perspective was something she desperately needed.

"I do want it." Meg pressed a hand to her belly. "And I appreciate you telling me everything. I know it wasn't easy."

He rolled his shoulders, stretching as he rotated his muscles. She watched the flex and bend, swallowing hard at the perfect specimen of masculinity he presented.

"It's in the past," he finally said.

Not so much, she wanted to tell him. But she didn't. Perspective, she reminded herself. She eased herself to a standing position, rubbing her arms, suddenly a little chilled now that the sun had set ... and reality had dawned with it. Facing the truth was a gift she was determined to give herself from now on.

"I'm going to head inside. I'm cold," she told him.

And where normally he'd wrap his arms around her and chase away the chill, he merely nodded. "I'll be up soon."

"I'll probably be asleep. It's been a really long day."

He didn't answer and she wasn't surprised. He was lost in thought, probably somewhere in the pain of his past. She wasn't as keen on thinking deeply or dwelling on what she couldn't change. She'd do as she'd told him. She'd turn in and hope she fell asleep. Tomorrow was a new day, and the way things were going, it would bring new challenges. Meg had to be ready to face them.

*   *   *

Scott headed indoors shortly after Meg went upstairs and popped open a cold beer. "What the hell are you doing?" he asked himself. Why had he let Meg go to bed alone when he knew how upset she had to be after his story? *Not the story, asshole*, but his gut reaction to what Leah had done.

That family thing is for suckers, and happily ever after only happens in fairy tales. What the fuck had possessed him to dump all that on her and in those words?

He rubbed his burning eyes with the heels of his hands. Meg had asked for honesty, and once he'd gotten rolling on what Leah had done, his lingering anger had burst through. He hadn't been talking to Meg. Sensitive, caring Meg. He'd been furious and still feeling betrayed by his ex-wife.

Scott put down the full bottle of beer. Drinking wasn't going to help. Neither was attempting to sort through his feelings for Meg, though he couldn't contain his thoughts.

He'd been unable to stay away from her, attraction and desire overcoming any rational thought. To be honest, he hadn't had a single rational moment since laying eyes on Meg in that hospital bed. As a result, he'd talked her into a one-night stand, though admittedly he hadn't had to try too hard to convince her. She'd been right there with him. Except he'd known going in that one night wouldn't be enough.

And now he found himself acting like her white knight and protector, and he had no regrets about it. None at all. The desire he'd felt for her from the beginning was still going strong, but now he *knew* her. Liked her even more.

Meg was everything Leah wasn't. Warm, caring, nurturing yet strong. Beautiful and real, inside and out. And she was more independent than she wanted to believe herself. He admired everything about her. But as much as he'd told himself he'd known she was pregnant going in, that it didn't matter, suddenly it did. She was creating a life for herself that he'd never believed he desired. And the one time he'd allowed himself to want it, everything had been ripped away from him in an instant, leaving him raw and back where he'd started. Convinced marriage, babies, and family weren't for him.

Except with Meg, a part of him was starting to envision just that, and it scared him to death. He couldn't pull away from her if he wanted to—and he didn't. Nor could he tell himself he was staying because she needed protection. He was sticking because he needed her. Wanted her. But Meg made it perfectly clear she preferred to be independent and not lean on any man. Which put him back in the same position he'd unwittingly found himself in with his ex.

When this mess with her stalker baby daddy was over, Meg might just decide she no longer needed *Scott* in her life. At all.

Carly Phillips

Chapter Eight

Meg woke up the next morning to find Scott wrapped around her, his big body curled around her back, one hand cupping her breast. Someone had put last night behind them, and she wished it were as easy for her. Still, nothing had changed between them, at least overtly. She was here until the threat was over, and neither of them had made any promises. If anything, his story and beliefs about the future merely reinforced her need to keep on as she had been. Planning an independent life on her own. But that didn't mean she couldn't enjoy the here and now.

His lips nuzzled at her neck, his breath warm, his touch electric. He pulled her closer and plucked at her nipple with one hand, turning her insides to liquid and making everything inside her melt with need.

She purred at the sensations pulsing straight to her core.

"You were asleep when I came in last night."

"I told you I probably would be."

He pinched her nipple tighter, and the current caused a trickle of dampness to settle between her thighs. "I'm making up for it this morning," he said, the head of his erection nudging at her opening.

"I can tell," she murmured, the last word falling off as he slid inside her body, which opened and eagerly accepted him. He was hot and hard, filling her up slowly and completely. "Ahh," she whispered, the sheer thickness of him pulsing inside her.

He rocked his hips back and forth, sheathing himself deeper, only to pull out and glide back in. "God, you feel good, Meg."

She closed her eyes, unable to fight the truth. "So do you."

He dipped his finger lower, moving from her breast to her clit, lubricating her with her own juices, his deft touch masterful. He always knew just how to play her to bring her to orgasm, but this wasn't the fast, furious sexual connection they normally shared.

His cock glided in and out of her almost reverently, his breathing growing ever rougher against her neck. Even the occasional talk was more intense and less dirty than usual, and she fell headlong into a glorious climax that was even more beautiful for the way he coaxed her through. Words like *so fucking beautiful, keep coming, baby*, and *it's my turn* echoing in her ears as his thrusts grew harder, his grip on her tighter as he came hard and fast inside her.

By the time their breathing had returned to normal, a big old lump had risen in her throat, and getting up to go to work hadn't been easy. Maybe Scott had recognized the intensity because he, too, had rolled away and said they should get ready for work.

For the rest of the week, they fell into a too-comfortable routine. Most times, Scott would leave first, knowing his brother made it a habit of getting into work early. Meg would leave soon after for school. When she left Scott's house, Rick would be waiting in his car and followed her. She was comforted knowing he was around and could handle Mike if he tried something or got violent. And with her thoughts and life in turmoil, she appreciated this little peace of mind.

Meg would get back to the house first, and because she was a guest, she wanted to help out. She'd had Rick accompany her to the grocery store so she could fill Scott's cabinets and fridge with food she could cook, and she had dinner waiting when he came home. Although she kept her mental dialogue going strong, reminding herself this situation was temporary, she couldn't deny how much she enjoyed being with him. It seemed like they fit into each other's lives well, from what they ate and when, to televisions shows and bedtime.

Unlike Mike and past boyfriends, Scott had no issues with the time she spent in the evenings, preparing her lessons for the kids. He was surprised that kindergarten wasn't just painting and crayons and seemed interested in what she planned for her class.

She couldn't deny that they not lived only together easily but that sex got better each time. She didn't understand it. Her prior relationships had been about making sure he got off or a quickie before bed. Scott's focus was solely on Meg's pleasure. If nothing else, he would be a hard act to follow when things ended.

He'd said as much himself, that fateful night on the patio. If he'd been thinking with his brain, he'd have recognized his relationship with his ex wouldn't last. Instead, he'd thought with his ... libido. And Scott had a healthy sex drive, as he'd proven over and over. What if Scott was thinking that way now, with Meg? What would happen when she started to show? She'd be popping soon, if the *What to Expect When You're Expecting* book was right. In fact, she could see the swell in her belly, even if he hadn't said a word. She'd only be getting bigger. No way would she be able to hold his interest sexually then.

Another depressing thought. But reality was her new friend, she reminded herself as she strode into school on Friday morning. After a morning teaching the letter *K*, Meg took her little charges to the art teacher, where they'd stay for the next forty minutes.

Before heading to the break room for coffee, she stopped at the office to check her mailbox and talk to Allie.

Meg hadn't had time with her friend since their girls' night, which felt like a lifetime ago, and she wanted to rectify that. She paused at the wall of small mailboxes and pulled out a few colored papers, notices, and other items before turning to her friend.

"Hi."

"Hi, yourself." Allie sat behind a metal desk and always greeted everyone with a warm smile.

"How are you feeling?" Allie gestured to Meg's stomach.

Meg blushed and grinned. "Pretty good, thanks. You?"

Allie shrugged. "Not bad. Listen, I need to talk to you," she said, lowering her voice.

"And I'd love to grab lunch sometime soon," Meg said. Allie was aware of the situation with Mike but not that she was living with Scott. They definitely had catching up to do.

"Great! I'll text you. I'm going to visit my parents this weekend, so maybe the next. But that's not what I wanted to talk about…"

"What is it?" Meg asked, concerned.

"Parents have been calling about a sedan in the parking lot with a driver sitting behind the wheel. Mr. Hansen went out to speak to the driver." Allie glanced over her shoulder at the partially open door, as if assuring they wouldn't be caught talking.

Meg's stomach cramped. "What happened?"

"The guy showed him an ID card from a protection agency and explained he was on the job for someone inside the school. He didn't mention names but..." Because Mr. Hansen, as well as Allie, knew Meg no longer wanted Mike allowed into the school...

"He put two and two together and came up with me as the person who needed protection," Meg said.

Allie inclined her head. "I'm so sorry."

"It's not your fault." Meg drew a deep gulp of air. "Does he want to see me?"

"Right away."

"Okay." Meg straightened her shoulders, ignored the nerves bouncing in her stomach, and strode around her friend's desk to the principal's office, knocking with her knuckles.

"Come in," he called.

She stepped in to find Mr. Hansen sitting behind his desk. He was a bland man, in personality and appearance. With his thinning black hair and plaid suits that had seen better days, it was obvious to Meg why she hadn't wanted to date him. There was zero attraction between them. The sun streamed in from behind him, the bright Florida sunshine in stark contrast to Meg's darkening mood.

"Good morning, Meg," he said, as always using her first name instead of the formality most principals preferred. "Please have a seat," he said in a serious tone.

She chose one of the two uncomfortable hard-backed chairs across from him.

"I'll get right to the point. I've had some phone calls from concerned parents about the man sitting outside the school in an unmarked car."

Meg gripped the edge of her chair harder. Of course she could comprehend why parents wouldn't be comfortable with a large man sitting in a black car, parked in the school lot for the entire day.

"I can explain."

"Then it does involve you?"

She closed her eyes and nodded.

"It was only conjecture until now."

Meg had known that, but she believed in owning up to her issues when confronted. "You already know I put my ex-boyfriend on a list of people I don't want to be allowed inside the school. The truth is, I have a restraining order against him," she admitted. She glanced down, noticed that her hands had begun to shake, and shoved them beneath her legs on the chair.

"Is the man dangerous?" Mr. Hansen asked. "Do I need to be concerned about the children?"

"Umm, he's only interested in me."

The other man narrowed his gaze. "What if the kids get in the way of him getting to you?"

Meg's mouth grew dry. "I didn't think... I wouldn't put the kids at risk." And she couldn't vouch for Mike's stability if he was drinking.

"I know you wouldn't do it deliberately, but that may be the end result. One of the parents who called is on the school board. She wants to call a meeting. She feels you should be suspended without pay, and frankly, given the situation, that's very likely how the board will vote."

Meg dipped her head, knowing what Mr. Hansen was getting at. She could go through with the farce of the board hearing, but the result was almost a given. If Meg had children in the school, knowing what she did about her ex, she'd vote to suspend her. What if Mike did become totally unhinged and was drinking and made a scene outside school? What if he went after her and the children were there? She shook her head, surprised she hadn't thought of this before. But she'd been so overwhelmed with things, she hadn't thought beyond her own problems.

"I understand," she whispered, her fear folding in

on her because she knew what was coming.

"Then we're in agreement. You'll take a voluntary suspension, and I'll explain things to the board."

Meg managed a nod as tears sprung to her eyes. Now she wasn't just an unwed mother, she was an unemployed, unwed mother with no income coming in. She'd counted on saving her money between now and when this school year ended for the new and unexpected baby-related expenses.

Somehow she rose to her feet on shaking legs and started for the door.

"Meg."

She turned and glanced over her shoulder. The sympathetic look on his face surprised her. "I really am sorry. I know how you feel about the children and them about you."

"Thank you."

She turned and headed out, walking past Allie with a half wave, unable to find the words to speak. Not without bursting into tears.

*   *   *

Scott spent the morning with Tyler, in a meeting with Lola Corbin. She came alone, no handlers or other band members with her. She was a pop star and music phenom, a woman who'd recently been voted sexiest woman alive by a men's magazine, yet she was clearly down-to-earth and ... normal despite her party-girl image. Most men would be salivating over her long dark hair, blue eyes, and killer body, but Scott preferred the brown-haired, brown-eyed schoolteacher he'd woken up to this morning.

He looked across the table at Lola, and after hashing out the security plans they'd implement if she hired them, Scott came to the conclusion that she knew how to handle her life. She didn't take shit from her bandmates, nor did she plan to let angry fans ruin her life. She was engaged to Peter Grissom, Jr., a Miami Thunder all-star player and another reason Tyler and Scott couldn't turn down the job. No matter how they felt about Grey Kingston.

They wrapped up the meeting with a firm commitment from Lola to hire them.

Scott's cell rang, and the screen showed Rick. "Talk to me."

"She just walked out of school, ignored me, got into her car, and drove off."

He glanced at his watch. They were barely halfway through the day. Was she sick? "Where is she headed?"

"Looks like your place."

"Okay, stick close to her. I'll be there soon. Thanks, man." Scott disconnected the call and dialed Meg, but it went straight to voice mail.

After a quick check-in with Tyler, Scott headed home, making the trip in record time. He acknowledged Rick, who sat in his vehicle on the street in front of the house, and pulled into his driveway, not surprised to find Meg's car already parked there.

He headed inside, not sure what to expect. "Meg?" He tossed his keys on the credenza by the front door.

When she didn't reply, he checked the kitchen and, finding it empty, headed for the bedroom. He found her lying on the bed, fully dressed, curled up on her side.

As much as he liked the sight of her on his bed, his stomach cramped with worry. "Hey." He sat down beside her on the mattress. "Are you sick?"

"Did Rick call and tattle on me?" she asked.

"He let me know you left work unexpectedly. You didn't answer your phone, so I came home to check on you."

She sniffed and pushed herself upright, then settled back against the pillows, her hair falling messily around her shoulders, makeup-streaked tears on her face. His stomach clenched at the sight.

"I'm not sick," she said, and he breathed freely for the first time since Rick's call.

She bit down on her lip, looking up at him with those big brown eyes. "But I am unemployed."

"Excuse me?"

"Parents called school to complain about the strange man in an unmarked car sitting on school property. The principal talked to Rick. He didn't give my name, but considering I'd put Mike on a list of people not to be allowed into the school, it wasn't difficult to figure out who he was guarding. One of the parents who complained is a board member, and she wanted to have a meeting." Meg rubbed her hands up and down her bare arms.

Scott was dying to pull her against him, but she didn't appear at all receptive at the moment. Unlike the time she'd thrown herself against him, she was stiff and unyielding, her body language screaming *don't touch*. She clearly didn't want to rely on him, and damn, but that hurt.

"How did that lead to you being fired?" he asked, sticking to facts.

"Unpaid leave," she said, enunciating each syllable. "The principal didn't force things. But when he asked me if Mike was a danger to the kids, I just didn't know. What if he showed up and was drinking? What if he got past Rick and the kids were in the way... I couldn't say for sure it was safe. And if it were my child, I'd want me gone." She shrugged in defeat. "There was no point in letting a board meeting happen, so I just accepted the inevitable."

Scott swore loudly. "I wish we could find the bastard, but according to Luke, Mike is MIA. We can't locate him, and he's spoken to friends and last-known coworkers. Any calls you've gotten have been on burner phones and are untraceable. But the Ashtons seem different." Scott needed to tell her more about what Luke had uncovered about the couple, but now wasn't the time.

"It doesn't matter. Mike's got the upper hand, just like he wants."

"Let's see if we can't tilt things in your favor. I think it's time to talk to Mike's parents. Let's see if they have any sway over their son."

"It didn't seem like it when I spoke to them, but it's worth a shot. I need this job," she said, her voice breaking. "I tried to think of alternatives. I can't tutor older kids to make money for the same reason I've basically been asked to leave. And I have savings, but I counted on my income to buy a crib and baby furniture, clothing, formula, diapers... I can't afford to let this situation go on."

Needing to touch her, hoping she needed contact with him too, he grasped her hands, threading their fingers together, the act meaning something to him. He pushed back the rush of panic and focused on the now. On Meg.

"We'll figure this out."

She glanced at him, her eyes glassy, her jaw set and

determined. "*I* will."

He absolutely noticed her use of the word *I*. Knew he'd caused it by his callous comment about family being for suckers and happily ever after happening only in fairy tales. A lump swelled in his throat, and everything inside him screamed at him to reassure her. To promise he'd be there for her no matter what. But rehashing his past had reminded him all too well of how much pain he'd been in when he'd lost his own baby. Which led to the horrible realization that if he allowed himself to think of Meg and the baby as *his*, and she walked away when the danger was over, he'd lose a lot more than he ever had with Leah.

And he didn't know if he could come back from that.

He glanced at Meg, noting both her fragility and the strength he admired. Damn, but he wished he'd thought this through earlier … like when he'd pushed for more than one night. But he hadn't. He'd let his desire for her win out and, as Meg had pointed out, his white knight complex to come out to play.

Fuck. Now neither one of them would escape this thing unscathed.

"Do you have the Ashtons' phone number?" he asked, focusing on her issues and not the emotions he couldn't control.

She nodded.

"Let's set up a meeting."

"Okay."

A phone call later and Meg had a plan to meet Mike's parents for brunch at an out-of-the-way restaurant in South Beach on Wednesday. He'd have preferred an immediate get-together, but they were out of town this weekend. Scott didn't know what, if anything, they could do to get their son under control, but assuming they cared about the baby the way they claimed to, he hoped they'd become Meg's allies. She deserved to have something in her life go right for once.

*   *   *

Meg woke up and slipped out of bed, leaving Scott fast asleep. After the craziness of yesterday, she'd barely remembered she had an OB/GYN appointment this morning. Her doctor worked one Saturday a month, and because Meg didn't want to miss a day of school, she'd taken a Saturday appointment. Now, of course, it didn't matter. But no matter now tired she was, she didn't want to skip something so important.

She took a quick shower, dressed, and slipped out of the bedroom, surprised Scott still slept soundly. She left him a note explaining where she went and propped it against the coffee machine, where he was most likely to see it first thing. She'd learned Scott liked his morning caffeine fix as soon as he woke up.

She had a hunch he wouldn't be happy she hadn't woken him and let him know she was headed out, but this was something she needed to do on her own. A doctor's appointment and sonogram of her baby was the most personal, intimate thing she could imagine, and though she longed to have someone to share it with—and that wasn't being needy, just honest—she understood she had to draw boundaries with Scott. No matter how much she wished otherwise, and there was no point denying that she did.

A quick glance told her that her friendly bodyguard sat outside the house, watching over her. Although Scott could handle things inside, Rick was making sure Mike didn't lurk or cause trouble outside. She pulled out of the driveway, slowed, and waved, giving him time to put the car in gear and follow. She wasn't stupid, nor would she take unnecessary chances. Mike was out there somewhere, not happy that she was still carrying his baby. Protection made sense.

A little while later, Meg lay on the table in a flimsy gown, and Dr. Taylor, a middle-aged woman who Meg trusted and liked a lot, spread warm gel over her belly.

"So we're going to find the heartbeat." The doctor moved the wand around while Meg held her breath. She vividly remembered the hospital visit after Mike had shoved her... She'd been bleeding, and the wait while the doctor searched for the heartbeat had been excruciating.

She felt that way now and found herself saying a little prayer, until finally, she heard the *whoosh, whoosh* from the machine. She expelled a long breath of relief.

"There we go," the doctor said cheerfully. "Nice and fast. Good job." She smiled and clicked on the screen, printing out the view. "Any questions for me this visit?" she asked.

Meg shook her head.

"You're taking your vitamins?"

"I am. They make me nauseous, but I try to do it after a meal."

"And that, too, is normal." She hooked her wand back into a holder and met Meg's gaze. "You look tired. Are you getting enough sleep?"

Meg swallowed hard. "Trying. I'm having some issues with the baby's father." She didn't want to go into detail. No point mentioning she was out of work for the moment as well.

"Well, stress isn't good for you or the baby," the doctor said, as if Meg needed the reminder. She wasn't asking for the nightmare her life had become.

"I know. There are just so many things that are out of my control right now."

"Well, I recommend you rest. You're healthy, but you did have that bleeding early on, and we don't want a repeat, right?"

"Right." Meg shifted uncomfortably on the hard examining table.

Dr. Taylor rose to her feet. "Everything looks good. Just try to take it easy," she said. "I'll see you next month. By then we should be able to see the sex of the baby, if you want to know ahead of time." She treated Meg to a warm smile. "Take care."

"Thank you," Meg murmured. She waited for the other woman to shut the door behind her before pulling herself up to a sitting position, clutching the paper gown around her.

Did she want to know the sex of the baby? She wasn't sure, but she had time to think about it. Her heart sped up at the thought of a little girl. Of course, she wanted a healthy baby and would adore a boy, but in her heart of hearts, she hoped she had a girl she could dress up and be there for. More than her own mom had been there for her, Meg thought sadly.

When she'd called her mother and told her about the pregnancy, Anne's response had been a succinct *well, that'll kill your chances of finding a good man.* Meg winced at the memory she'd tried hard to push far, far away. Was that how her mother felt about her? That once her dad had left, Meg had been a burden and in the way of her finding her prince? Heaven knew, she never had.

Meg dressed and drove home, trying her best not to dwell on sad or negative thoughts. As the doctor had pointed out, she didn't need added stress in her life.

It helped when Luke called to fill her in about his search on Mike's parents. On paper, at least, they weren't the monsters Mike had painted them out to be. Although Meg needed to know more, along with time to digest what she'd learned, she calmed a bit about meeting them.

She walked into the house and headed straight for the kitchen, where she found Scott sitting with her note and a cup of coffee in front of him. Razor stubble covered his handsome face.

He wore a tee-shirt, a pair of track pants, and his feet were bare. Her mouth watered at the sexy picture he presented.

"Good morning," she said, setting her purse, keys, and the sonogram photograph on the table.

"How was your appointment?" he asked.

She shrugged. "Everything's fine."

"Are you sure?" he asked gruffly.

"Why wouldn't it be? Can I get you more coffee?" she asked, changing the subject.

"No thanks." He stared into the mug, his expression unreadable. "I'm fine."

He didn't sound fine, but she couldn't read what

was bugging him. Surely he hadn't wanted to go with her to the doctor. That thought was ridiculous in the extreme.

He picked up the picture and stared at the small black-and-white photo.

She wrapped her hand around the top of the nearest chair and gripped it hard. "It's hard to really see anything," she said, suddenly uncomfortable.

Scott stared at the sonogram picture. He'd seen one before, when one of the guys at the station was passing it around like a proud dad. His ex had never brought one home to show him.

Looking at Meg's baby had his insides twisting with so many conflicting emotions it was hard to name them all. But the one that stuck out, the most surprising one, was longing.

He placed the picture back on the table. "You didn't have to go alone."

She pinned him with a surprisingly steady, certain gaze. "Yes, I did." She paused, as if waiting for him to say more. When he didn't, she straightened her shoulders. "Look, I really appreciate everything you're doing for me. And I'm … enjoying what we have."

She sounded so blasé. Words like *enjoy* and *appreciate* didn't come close to the feelings she churned up inside of him. When he'd woken up to find her side of the bed empty, no Meg to wrap himself around, he'd been thrown. Which showed him how quickly he'd gotten used to having her in his life. And when he'd found her note in the kitchen, he'd been ... hurt that she'd gone to her appointment alone. He didn't understand the feelings, couldn't figure out what to do with them, but there they were.

"Scott, are you listening?" she asked.

"Yes." He didn't like what he was hearing, but he was definitely listening.

"Okay." She licked her lips nervously. "Well, I was saying, I really think it's better if we keep the personal separate from—"

"From what?" He rose and stepped into her *personal* space, deliberately crowding her.

He needed to be close, to touch her, to inhale her scent and feel that his world was set right again. Dammit, she tied him in knots.

The minute he crowded her, her words trailed off. Her eyes dilated, her breathing slowed, and she swallowed hard, the action causing her throat to move up and down. He had the sudden desire to kiss her there, to run his teeth along her silken skin.

But she was making a point. One he didn't like. She'd put him on edge, and there was only one outlet that would make him feel better. But first they had to get a few things straight.

"You'd like to separate the personal from the ...

what?" he asked, his voice dark. He heard the warning in his tone.

"Sex," she said on a rush. "You couldn't possibly have wanted to go with me to the doctor this morning, so I didn't wake you. Now you're acting all hurt and pissed off, and I don't get it."

"Join the club, baby. I don't get it either. But you make me crazy. You make me want things I shouldn't, things that will come back and bite me in the ass in the end. But it doesn't stop me from wanting."

He grasped her arms and hauled her against him, sealing his lips over hers. Her hands came to his shoulders, and for a brief second, he thought she'd push him away. Then her hands curled into his shirt, her lips softened, and she gave herself over to the kiss and to him.

Chapter Nine

Not only could Meg not resist Scott, she couldn't resist how much he wanted her. His torment called to hers. They might not know what they were doing relationship-wise, but *this*, they knew how to do well.

The kiss was hard and demanding, full of the same frustration she'd sensed in him when she'd walked in, but he tasted so good, a hint of coffee and all Scott, as he plundered her mouth.

His hand went for the waistband of her pants, and he yanked them down, his big hand cupping her sex. "So fucking hot and wet," he groaned.

She arched into his touch, and he pushed her panties aside and immediately thrust one finger deep inside, curling into her and finding her sweet spot immediately. Small tremors kicked in without warning, and a low, vibrating moan escaped her throat.

"I love how responsive you are." He buried his

face in her neck and sucked along her collarbone, all the while pumping one finger in and out until she was a writhing mess of need.

Oh God. She was *this* close to coming, and when he pressed his thumb over her clit, rubbing her as his finger did its thing, she shattered into pieces, warm, beautiful waves of bliss pulling her under. Only Scott's strong arm around her back kept her on her feet.

As she came back to herself, he was shoving his pants down and kicking them away. Before she could remove her panties, he slid them down her shaking legs. She could barely process where they were or what was happening, some small part of her knowing this wasn't a bedroom. But he picked her up, and she wrapped her legs around him, and he strode to the couch in the next room and stood her on her feet.

"Turn around," he said in a gruff but oh-so-sexy voice.

She spun immediately, allowing him to bend her over the arm of the sofa. Her full breasts pressed against the cushioned material as he grasped her hips and maneuvered her hips and legs where he wanted them.

Excitement pulsed through her veins as the head of his erection nudged her already-slick opening, gliding partway into her with ease. He teased her with his cock, little pumps in and out, never quite embedding himself all the way in. Her sex clenched and squeezed around him, trying to capture and pull him all the way home, so she could feel him, thick and pulsing, deep inside. But he maintained the arousing thrusts, and her desire built with crazy speed.

He rested one hand on her lower back and suddenly slowed his hips, tracing her vertebrae slowly with his calloused but gentle hand. "So pretty," he said, almost to himself, but the words, spoken in awe, wrapped around her heart.

She dipped her head forward and moaned, wondering how she was supposed to resist falling for this man. If he was all gruff, demanding, alpha, she could keep her walls high, but the tender, unexpected gestures caused her to trip further over that forbidden line, and a lump formed in her throat.

"You ready, baby?" He gripped her hips with both hands, his tight hold causing a painful rush of arousal in her sex.

"Beyond," she managed to choke out, her empty body craving his. Her heart needing him even more.

No. She pushed that awful, scary thought aside.

And when he thrust deep inside her, deeper than she'd ever felt him before, she stopped thinking at all. He groaned, low and deep, and she felt it everywhere in the best possible ways.

"Are you okay?" he asked, surprising her. "The last

thing I want to do is hurt you." He smoothed his hand over her backside, and she turned to meet his gaze.

"You wouldn't hurt me intentionally, Scott. And you aren't hurting me now." Later was probably another story, but she couldn't do anything to stop it. "But if you don't move … *now*, I'm going to hurt you." And with that, she thrust her hips back against him.

With a low chuckle, he proceeded to do as she asked, taking her hard while still holding back, she could tell. It didn't matter when he knew just how to make love to her, to find that right spot and send her soaring. He followed after her, and the hot feel of him coming inside her, her name on his lips, echoing in her ears, was something she'd never forget.

*   *   *

A little while later, Meg had showered and was making lunch in the kitchen. Scott had retreated to his office, a masculine room with wooden shelves and a large-screen computer set up at his desk. Meg wasn't stupid; she was well aware something between them had shifted from easy to hard, sex being the one thing they seemed to get right. He was obviously fighting feelings that he didn't want to deal with, either because he was just against marriage and a family in his future or the fact of her pregnancy had finally set in.

She chopped up lettuce and vegetables for a salad,

tossed in some grilled chicken, and added dressing.

She was about to call Scott in for lunch when her phone rang.

She glanced down, happy to see Olivia's name on the screen, and answered immediately. "Hi!" she said.

"Hi yourself. How was your appointment today?" Olivia asked.

"Everything's status quo. The doctor asked if I wanted to know the sex of the baby," she said as she washed her hands and put the big bowl of salad on the table.

"Do you want to know what you're having?" Olivia asked. "Because I want to be surprised."

Meg sighed. "I'm so torn. On the one hand, knowing will make the buying easier. On the other, I want to experience the newness and surprise."

Olivia laughed. "I hear you. I have so many things on order I'm afraid to figure out how to get it all home."

Meg tried to ignore the pang of envy at how easy it seemed for Olivia. The man who loved her, the money to do what she needed for her child. The grass always looked greener, but it wasn't necessarily the case. Although for Olivia and Dylan, Meg truly hoped it was. They deserved every bit of happiness.

So do you, a little voice in her head told her, but she pushed it aside. What you deserved and what life threw at you were often vastly different. "I'm just about to eat lunch. Can I call you back?" Meg asked.

"Sure. But I'll see you tonight?" Olivia asked.

"What's tonight?"

An awkward silence followed, and then Olivia said, "My mom asked all the kids to come for dinner. I just thought... Never mind. Call me later." Olivia rushed off the phone, and Meg didn't blame her.

She turned and caught sight of Scott standing in the doorway, watching her. "You scared me!"

"Sorry. I didn't want to interrupt your call."

"No problem. I was just going to get you anyway. Lunch is ready."

"Thank you. Looks good. And I appreciate it."

"It's fine."

He stepped into the kitchen. "Listen, my mother called a few minutes ago. She wants us all at the house for dinner tonight at six. She has an announcement of some sort."

"That's fine. I can keep busy here." She stepped over to one of the cabinets and pulled out glasses.

"Actually, I was hoping you'd come with me."

She met his serious gaze. "It sounds like it's a family thing." Not only didn't she belong there, she didn't want anyone getting the wrong idea of what was going on between her and Scott.

"My mom's been with this guy, Michael Brooks,

for a few years. I just have an uneasy feeling. I don't know what she has to say, and I'd like you there when I hear it," he said, his gaze softening as he looked at her. "Her boyfriend's a decent guy, but it'll be weird to hear if she's going to remarry. She's been through enough."

"You think marrying him would be bad for her?" Meg asked, wondering if this was more of Scott's negative views on family and marriage or if he had a legitimate issue with his mother's boyfriend.

He rolled his shoulders, obviously uncomfortable with the question. "Probably not. It's still just weird having another guy with my mother," he said. "I hate what my father did to her but…"

Taking her by surprise, he slid his fingers into hers, clasping them tightly together. "Like I said, it's awkward, and I'd really like you with me."

Her heart swelled, her throat feeling full at his admission. It was the admission of the young boy inside him, not the man he was now, and she was touched he'd let her in. He'd done so much for her. How could she be selfish and fight him on this?

Even if meeting his mother and the rest of his family felt too intimate and a lot awkward for her, she could put her own feelings aside and be there for him for a change.

"Okay," she said softly. "I'll come with you."

"Thank you." The look he gave her was enough to send her running far and fast, but she was in this.

Until he no longer was.

*   *   *

Meg's heart was in her throat as Scott pulled up to his mother's house in Weston and parked the truck. It was an imposing yet gorgeous structure with tropical shrubbery, a circular driveway, and acreage, which was unusual in Florida. A variety of luxury cars filled the drive, letting her know that many of his siblings had already arrived.

"Relax." He placed his hand over hers, which were entwined together, as she'd been twisting them nervously in her lap.

"I really don't belong here."

"Hey," he said, his voice strong and sure. Calming even. "I want you here. That means you belong."

She knew that in her head, but her heart was beating way too fast inside her chest.

"You're doing this for me, and I appreciate it." He slid his hand behind her neck, pulled her close, and sealed his mouth over hers, effectively shutting her up. He kissed her hard and long, until the pounding inside her body had nothing to do with nerves and everything to do with the heat and desire he generated. He nibbled on her lower lip before releasing her with a

194

strangled groan, pausing to catch his breath by resting his forehead against hers.

"Better?" he asked.

She couldn't stop the smile curving her lips. "Much."

He shook his head and laughed. "Stick with me. I know what you need."

She pulled down the visor to check her makeup. Not much she could do about her puffy lips, but the rest of her was okay.

"You're beautiful, Meg."

He spoke so softly and reverently she believed he meant that. "Thank you." Blowing out a puff of air, she picked up the pie she'd insisted they stop and buy. "I'm ready."

A chic-looking woman met them at the door, her dark hair with soft highlights falling around her face. From their similar features, Meg knew immediately she was Scott's mother.

"Scott, honey, it's so good to see you." She pulled him into a warm hug.

"Hey, Mom."

"And you must be Meg! I'm so glad you could join us." Her warmth was genuine. The sparkle in her eyes could be mistaken for nothing except happiness.

"Thank you. I hope I'm not intruding."

"Nonsense. I was thrilled when Scott told me he

was bringing a guest." Emma accepted the bakery box from Meg. "Thank you so much. You didn't need to bring anything, but extra sweets are always welcome." She ushered them into the house, and Scott shot Meg an *I told you it would all be okay* look.

Yes, fine. The man had been right again.

He placed a strong hand on her back and led her toward the sound coming from inside the house. The gesture was meant to be reassuring, but every time he touched her, he lit Meg's body on fire. The chemistry between them was that potent and hot.

She smoothed her hand over the dress she'd chosen, glad she'd been able to fit into her favorite one, though barely. No need to break out the maternity wear for tonight.

They stepped into a large state-of-the-art kitchen that was open and led to a great room, where the rest of the family had gathered.

"Meg!" Olivia's familiar voice sounded above the others. Meg walked toward her friend, while Scott stopped to talk to Ian and Riley, who Meg greeted with a wave. She'd catch up with her later.

Olivia greeted Meg with a big hug. "So glad you're here too!"

Meg hugged her back but didn't reply.

She glanced up and saw Dylan, waiting for his hello, a smile on his face. "Hey, Meggie."

"Dylan! It's been a long time." They embraced like old friends.

It had been awhile since she'd spoken to Dylan. These days when she needed an ear, she was more likely to call one of her girlfriends or Olivia than her old friend. And that seemed to work fine for them both.

"Oh! Avery's here. I'll be back in a few," Olivia said, rushing off to talk to her sister.

"You look good," Dylan said, holding on to her hand. "And Olivia keeps me up on how you're doing."

"It's been … interesting, to say the least."

"You're handling everything, just like I knew you would."

"Well, I have help …" She trailed off, afraid Dylan would think she was falling back into old patterns, relying on a man when she should be handling things herself. "It's not the same this time," she rushed to tell him. "Scott's helping me professionally. I really don't know how I'd handle Mike practically stalking me if not for him."

And she didn't feel like she was latching on to him the same way she had with men in her past. Whatever her feelings for him, they were more solid and real. Even if he'd made it clear they couldn't go anywhere.

"Relax, Meg. I'm not judging you," Dylan assured her.

As her one-time boyfriend, later best friend, Dylan knew her insecurities and tendencies better than most. He was the one who'd called her on her behavior when warranted. He was also the one who would never abandon her if she really needed him. The amazing thing was, since he'd drawn the line in their relationship, she really hadn't needed him at all. Not the way she'd once thought.

"Maybe I am. My life is just spinning out of control. But at the same time, I'm thinking clearly and trying to keep things in perspective."

He smiled at that. "Good."

She shrugged. "That's it? No words of advice?"

He brushed at his goatee with his fingers. "I don't think you need them. Not from me," he said at the same moment a solid arm slipped around Meg from behind.

"Am I interrupting?" Scott asked, an unusual edge to his voice.

"No. I was just telling Meg that pregnancy agrees with her," Dylan said smoothly, avoiding mentioning anything personal in their conversation. Scott wouldn't appreciate knowing they'd been talking about him, even in a roundabout way.

"Yes, it does." Scott squeezed her waist and pressed an unexpected kiss to her cheek. "I'm going to steal her away now," he informed Dylan, who stepped back immediately.

Meg narrowed her gaze, surprised there wasn't more pleasant conversation between the two men.

"Time to meet the rest of the clan," Scott said, leading her away from Dylan before she could manage a reply.

She spun out of his embrace. "What was that about?"

"Just—"

"Staking a claim? He's married to your sister, for God's sake."

Scott blew out a long breath. "And he's crazy about her. I know. Shit."

She narrowed her gaze. "What is it?"

He grasped her hand and pulled her to an empty, small study, decorated in dark colors, a leopard carpet on the floor and gold accessories on the wooden built-in shelves.

He pushed the door partially closed. "I don't know what that was. I saw you with Dylan, knew he was the only guy you were really in love with, and I went a little crazy."

Jealous? Scott had been jealous of Dylan? Her eyes opened wide at his admission. "Dylan and I haven't been together since high school," Meg said, speaking softly because no way did she want anyone overhearing.

"Yeah, well, before me, he was the one you turned to for everything. And that wasn't all that long ago."

Meg searched for the words to explain, knowing it wouldn't be easy. "A few short months ago, I would have sworn Dylan and I were just friends. That he was my best friend and I was his."

"And now?" he asked, his jaw tight.

"Now I can look back and say my need for Dylan wasn't healthy. It wasn't a two-sided friendship. I was … clingy, needy, and to be honest, it embarrasses me." She refused to duck from Scott's heated gaze. He needed to hear this, and she needed to say it.

She reached up and stroked his cheek, wanting to ease his distress. She felt the rasp of razor stubble beneath her fingers and loved the feel of his skin against hers.

"And that's why you're so afraid of leaning on anyone?"

"Partly. I don't want to be that person who can't take care of herself."

She also didn't want to fall apart when this thing between them ended. Even before she understood his feelings on marriage and family, she'd worried that she wasn't enough to make him stay. Or worse, that she would come to be too much of a burden and drive him away. None of that mattered now. He was going no matter what.

"Scott?" a female voice called out. "Olivia told me you were here, and I want to meet Meg... There you are!" A pretty woman with long dark hair walked in, stopping short. "Oh, sorry! I didn't mean to interrupt a private conversation."

"No, come in," Meg said brightly. "Are you Avery?"

The other woman nodded. "Hi, Scott." She pecked him on the cheek. "It's great to meet you," she said, turning to Meg. "Olivia has told me so much about you. We have to all get together for girls' night. I can drink, and you two pregnant women can watch me drown my sorrows," she said, following up with an obviously forced smile.

"Av, are you okay?"

"I'm great!"

Even Meg knew her words were forced and wondered what was bothering her.

"I'd love to chat and get to know you, but Mom said it's dinnertime, so we need to go into the dining room." Avery spun around and walked out of the room.

"What's going on with her?" Meg asked Scott.

He groaned. "I think it has something to do with an old boyfriend." Scott explained that Grey Kingston of the band Tangled Royal was Avery's high school boyfriend. "He left her to go find fame and fortune, which he did. According to Olivia, he called her last time he was in town, and they got together. Nobody knows what happened, but she's been … off ever since."

"Scott! Dinner!" someone called.

He shot Meg a wry grin. "Let's go find out what my mother's big news is."

Meg had to hand it to Emma, she had a flair for the dramatic, ignoring her children's questions throughout dinner and holding her news for after dessert.

"So I'm sure you all wonder why I asked you to come here tonight," Emma finally said.

"Been wondering, Mom," Avery said.

"I think I know," Olivia said next with a grin.

"Not playing twenty questions," Ian muttered to his sisters. "Let's hear it."

"Well, Michael wanted to be here, but he had a work emergency, which is just as well because I wanted to talk to all of you alone."

Meg squirmed in her seat, feeling very much like an outsider. As if sensing her emotions, Scott reached for her beneath the table, his hand coming to rest on her thigh, squeezing lightly. The act calmed her, then immediately spiked her pulse, but she forced herself to focus on his mother's words.

"Michael asked me to marry him and I said yes."

The women around the table squealed, called out congratulations, and Emma's daughters jumped up to hug her. The men, Scott and his brothers in particular, sat in stunned silence. Which was what Meg sensed had had Emma so concerned. And why she was glad her fiancé hadn't been able to make this family dinner.

Meg immediately slid her hand over Scott's, giving him silent support, as she knew he'd been dreading something like this. Having never met Michael, she couldn't judge Emma's taste in men or why her sons were so concerned.

"Isn't this a little soon?" Ian spoke up first, his dark tone silencing the women's excitement.

Emma turned her gaze toward her oldest son. "Funny you should ask that. Michael and I have been together now … for about as long as you and Riley," she said pointedly. "And my granddaughter is asleep in a crib upstairs. "Any other objections?" she asked, her voice strong.

But the wobble of her chin and the sheen of tears in her eyes told a whole different story. She might be a grown woman, but she desperately wanted her family's approval. Meg didn't blame her. Though she didn't know what it was like to have such a large family, with everyone having differing opinions and feelings, Meg envied this group their closeness.

"He's a nice guy, but do you have to marry him?"

Scott asked. "It's just so permanent, and what if things don't work out?"

"Are you saying you don't believe in marriage anymore?" Olivia asked her brother.

"Goddammit, Liv, this isn't about me," Scott snapped back.

That was too close to the conversation they'd had about his feelings on family, and Meg slipped lower into her chair. She didn't know how many gut-punching reminders she could take.

"He's good to her," Olivia said to Ian, but the sweep of her gaze encompassed all her brothers. "You've all seen it. What do you want? For Mom to be alone for the rest of her life? Dad's not. He's off doing what's best for him. He always has. Why does he deserve to get what he wants out of life with Savannah but Mom doesn't?" She wrapped an arm around her mother's shoulder.

"Okay, everyone, stop. Right now," Emma said. "I called you all here to give you the courtesy of letting you know. I wasn't asking your permission. I'd like it if you could all be happy for me. If not, then at least shut up about it." Emma's voice cracked, and Scott jumped out of his seat, followed by Ian and Tyler, who'd sulked in silence.

"I guess it's just that no one's good enough," Scott said gruffly as he reached her. "I love you. Michael's a good guy. I'm happy for you."

Or he'd get there, Meg thought, her heart too wrapped up in his feelings and this family drama. She really needed to get out of here and breathe. Except leaving here meant going to Scott's house, not her own. She pulled in a shaky breath, watching as everyone now congratulated Emma and made their peace with her decision. Meg was the last to step up and offer her good wishes.

Then finally it was time to leave. Exhaustion beat at every bone in Meg's body. She couldn't wait to go to sleep.

Olivia caught up with Meg before she made it to the front door. "Are you okay?" Olivia asked.

"Why wouldn't I be? I feel bad that your family isn't all supportive of your mom, but I'm sure they'll get there."

Olivia smiled. "They will. The guys are ... guys. But I'm talking about you."

"Nothing to worry about," Meg lied. No reason to involve his sister in her feelings for Scott.

"Okay, well, I wanted to know if you and Scott were up for dinner tomorrow night. You know, the four of us. I think it'd be fun."

Meg blinked, surprised. "Oh, umm ... I don't know. Scott might be busy." Not that he tended to go out at night, but a couple's date when she and Scott weren't really in a formal relationship?

"I'm not busy, and dinner sounds good to me," Scott said, coming up behind her.

"Great!" Olivia said. "One of you call me in the morning, and we'll pick a place and time. I'm going to check on Mom."

Once they were in the truck headed home, Scott glanced at her, one hand resting on the steering wheel as he drove. "Any reason you were trying to avoid going out with them?" he asked, way too perceptive as usual.

She figured honesty was the best way to handle this. "For the same reason I'm trying to get you to see that I'm here for security reasons only. I know we're sleeping together, but that's because we can't seem to keep our hands off each other."

He grinned. "You've got that right."

She shook her head. "I just don't want to give your family the wrong impression," she said.

"And what impression would that be?" he asked.

She wondered why he was deliberately being so dense. "That we're a couple with any long-term potential," she said.

"Well, thank you for being so blunt. Now I know you're only in it for sex," he said, sounding grumpy and put out, when he was the one, more than her, who didn't believe in anything else.

She raised an eyebrow at that. "And you're not? Or are you lining up for labor, delivery, and daddy duty?"

When he didn't answer, she glanced out the passenger window and remained silent for the rest of the ride.

By the time they arrived at Scott's, neither one of them was up for much in the way of conversation or anything else, for that matter. She washed up in his luxurious bathroom that was three times the size of her own and climbed into his bed.

Long after Scott pulled her into his arms and drifted off to sleep, Meg's thoughts were churning around in her head. As was Olivia's shouted question at Scott.

Are you saying you don't believe in marriage anymore? his sister had asked.

Or are you lining up for labor, delivery, and daddy duty?

She squeezed her eyes shut tight, wishing she didn't care about his refusal to answer either question.

Chapter Ten

Scott dressed for dinner, listening to the sound of Meg getting ready in his bathroom. The low hum of the blow-dryer and the small sounds of different jars and items being placed on the marble countertops. Sounds that were becoming all too familiar and comfortable. He hated how strained things were between them now. He missed the days when they could say and do anything without thought or consequence.

He buttoned his shirt, chosen because Emilio's was a nice restaurant. No tee shirts there. It was located near his half brother Alex's apartment in an out-of-the-way location. So as not to run into Alex and Madison and have them feel slighted, Scott had texted Alex and asked if the other couple wanted to join them, but they had other plans. Alex promised to get in touch, and they could do something another time. Scott refused to think about whether or not that time would come. Where Meg would be in a few short weeks.

She stepped out of the bathroom, and Scott sucked in a shallow breath at the sight of her. Her hair fell over one shoulder in soft waves, and her skin had burned slightly during her afternoon in the sun while he'd been holed up in his home office. Her cheeks were flushed pink, her brown eyes highlighted in a soft purple, her lips a lush shimmer he wanted to taste. Now.

She stared at him, her gaze hesitant after this afternoon's distance, and he didn't blame her.

"You look gorgeous," he said, breaking the silence and, he hoped, any tension.

He couldn't stop staring. She wore a one-piece white outfit that set off her tan, with flowing pants and a ruffled layer that cut straight across her lush chest. He didn't miss the fact that her breasts were getting bigger … and more sensitive.

Hell, all of her was more responsive, to his hands, his mouth and, yes, even his cock. Her body accepted him easily, clasping him in amazing heat and shattering more easily each time. At this point, he was willing to concede prowess to her hormones, he thought wryly, not that he was complaining in the least. He just wished the emotions between them weren't such a minefield, laden with unforeseen traps and triggers.

"Thank you," Meg said. Her gaze raked over him, and a soft smile pulled at her lips. "You look pretty good yourself."

He glanced at his black pants and white long-sleeve button-down and shrugged. "I shaved earlier."

She laughed and the sound lightened the mood. "Then that's it, I guess."

"Ready for dinner?"

"I'm starving," she said.

He frowned. "That's because you missed lunch."

"I had a shake a little while ago." She picked up a small straw purse. "All set," she told him.

He hooked his arm in hers and led her down to his truck. He helped her into the seat, ignoring the feel of her waist in his hands, swallowing a groan. He slammed her door shut and headed around to the driver's side.

The trip to Miami passed quickly, music on the radio, easy conversation around them. This was what he'd missed, he thought. Although they hadn't been together long, their first weeks had been so easy. Had he ever been with another woman who fit him so well? Thank goodness that thought hit just as he pulled up to the parking lot near Emilio's and he pulled down his window to deal with the attendant.

A few minutes later, they were seated across from Olivia and Dylan in the small Italian restaurant. Olivia had made a reservation, and Anna had reserved them a private table in the corner. His sister had already ordered sparkling water. Dylan and Scott passed on hard alcohol. They ordered quickly, Olivia asking Emilio to serve slowly so they had time to relax and talk.

Talk made Scott nervous, especially when his sister was involved, but Meg and Olivia had developed a close friendship in a short time, so he hoped the women would carry the more intense parts of conversation.

Scott knew exactly what had him on edge. Olivia was intuitive and would notice any problems. His sister had already warned him about hurting Meg, and looking back, Scott should have listened harder. Thought more. If Dylan got a whiff of tension tonight, he'd be in even more trouble.

To make matters worse, his sister couldn't be trusted not to dig into private, personal conversations better left alone. Especially when it came to his love life. Knowing how much Olivia cared about Meg, he could only hope she was smart tonight.

They started with football, a conversation that was always fun and easy, and segued into Scott's new position within Tyler's firm.

"I'm enjoying the freedom involved, catching up on client files and getting to know what everyone needs. It's been challenging on a whole different level," Scott explained.

"I bet," Dylan said. "It's great to do something you enjoy." As travel director for the Thunder, Dylan knew what he was talking about. The man loved his job. "Meg, how are things at school? Kids still keeping you on your toes?" Dylan asked.

And just like that, easy conversation ground to a halt.

"Umm, I—" Meg stammered.

"Meg is fine," Scott said, hoping to help Meg bypass the answer entirely.

"Actually I'm not. I'm on temporary leave," Meg said, going on to explain how the situation that her ex had escalated, leading to the principal strongly suggesting she take leave.

"Oh my God! Why didn't you say anything?" Olivia asked. "I'd have come over ... called, something," she said, offering all the support she could.

"I'm going to kill the bastard," Dylan said, his hands curling into fists.

"Well, get in line, because when *I* find him, he's going to wish he'd never been born." Though Scott appreciated Dylan backing Meg, when it came to protecting her, *he* wanted that job and didn't mind letting the other man know it.

Olivia studied him, eyes narrowed, and Scott swallowed a curse.

"I don't want anyone confronting Mike for me. He's dangerous," Meg said. "But I'm meeting with his parents on Wednesday."

"*We're* meeting with his parents," Scott reminded her.

Meg raised an eyebrow. "I was going to discuss that with you in the morning. I think it's better if I go alone. Rick will keep an eye on me."

Scott tensed, clenching his jaw and wondering when things had spiraled out of his control. "We'll talk about it when we're alone," he said, well aware of Dylan's and Olivia's intense stares, taking in every word and action that Meg and Scott made.

"Well, regardless, I'm not worried about meeting with them anymore. Luke said the background check turned up all good things. Lydia and Walter seem to be rational, decent people. They support children's charities and—"

"What the hell do you know about what Luke found?" Scott asked her. Everything about Meg's case was supposed to be his domain. Luke had no right to jump in with answers Scott had planned to give her, and he'd intended to have this conversation in the morning before the lunch meeting.

Meg merely shrugged, ignoring his sharp tone. "Luke called earlier today. *He* filled me in."

"I was going to tell you everything. There just hasn't been time."

Dylan braced his arms on the table. "Meggie, I can't imagine one good thing about the people who raised that asshole," he said skeptically.

At the old nickname Dylan called her, Scott's jaw locked in place.

"Actually, it's not what you think," Meg said to Dylan. "The Ashtons adopted Mike when he was a baby. I didn't know that. He also had fetal alcohol syndrome, so there's that component too. I suppose I can't necessarily blame them for how Mike turned out. There's definitely something to genetics."

She trembled as she spoke, and Scott could guess where her mind had gone. His anger fled in the face of her obvious fears. He knew for sure what she was thinking.

"Don't think that way." He settled his hand over hers, hoping to comfort her. "Your baby will be fine even with that bastard's genes. He has *you*." And a deep-seated longing arose inside him because he wanted to claim that position in the baby's life too.

Shit. He was in so much trouble.

"Meg, are you okay?" Olivia asked softly.

Scott glanced her way.

Her eyes looked suspiciously damp. "Actually, I'm going to go to the ladies' room. Excuse me."

Scott rose as she stood and headed for the other side of the restaurant.

He lowered himself back into his seat.

"Scott, what the hell is going on?" Olivia asked.

"I'd like an answer to that too," Dylan said.

Emilio walked over with food in his hands, and Olivia waved him away. "A few minutes, please?"

The older man nodded.

"Talk fast, big brother," she muttered.

"Shit. Everything was fine until I told her about Leah."

Olivia glanced at Dylan. "His ex-wife. I told you about her," she said.

Dylan nodded. "What about her?" he asked, his tone chilly.

"It's not about her, it's about what she did. Before her, I didn't want kids. When she got pregnant, I got excited. Invested. I really wanted to be a father. But she never came around, and instead of talking about it with me, she had an abortion. Just like that, everything I'd dreamed about was gone." He snapped his fingers in the air. "Telling Meg reminded me of the pain, and I said something stupid."

Dylan narrowed his gaze.

In for a penny, Scott thought. "I said, the whole family thing is for suckers, and happily ever after only happens in fairy tales." He ducked his head and groaned. "I pretty much put any nail in the coffin of whatever was happening between us."

"So explain you don't feel that way anymore!" Olivia glanced over her shoulder, but there was no sign of Meg yet.

"What if I do?"

"Excuse me?" his sister asked, sounding appalled.

"Look, Liv," he said, ignoring Dylan because he really couldn't deal with the other man at the moment. "I love her, okay? What if I let myself get so involved with her and the baby and then we wrap things up with her stalker ex and she doesn't need me anymore? She can pick up and move out, and that's it. Everything gone again. Except this time, I don't know if I'd get over it."

His sister's jaw had gone slack. "You love her?"

Scott couldn't believe he'd said it out loud either. Hell, he hadn't admitted it to himself before now. But what else was this driving need to be with her, to protect her, to get so involved in her life that she wouldn't want to leave?

"Yeah, I do."

"Then man up," Dylan said.

Scott clenched his hands beneath the table. "What the fuck do you know about me or my life?" he asked the other man. "Just because you are or were Meg's best friend doesn't give you the right to tell me what to do."

Dylan's hand came down on the table hard. Olivia jumped, then wrapped her fingers around his hand. "Stop it and listen. Both of you."

She turned to Scott. "I, of all people, know how hard it is to get over the pain in your past."

His sister had lost a baby when she was young, been betrayed by both that baby's father and their own parent. So yes, Olivia understood better than most.

"But the risk is so worth it," she said, glancing at her husband, her eyes shining with love. "Dylan stuck by me. He never gave up on me. On us. And because of that, I was able to come around and believe that I deserved a future that included kids ... and a good man," she said, her voice thick and full of emotion.

His sister's words wrapped around him, making sense not because of the logic but due to the fact that she'd all but experienced the same feelings of loss. She'd closed herself off to more. And she'd come out the other side because she'd been brave.

"Look, man. You knew Meg was pregnant when you started this thing. Are you really going to bail now because it's getting real?"

"Dylan," Olivia said, warning him to shut up with her tone.

"What? It's the truth," Dylan muttered.

"He gets what I said, don't you?" his sister asked

him.

Scott met Olivia's gaze and nodded, because he did. Olivia had done what he would have thought was impossible and gotten through to him. Dylan was right. He had to man up. Not necessarily throw Meg's life into further turmoil by dumping his feelings on her in the middle of her current nightmare, but he had to stop waffling. He'd told her from the beginning he was all in.

Then he'd turned around and backed off when messy emotions had gotten involved. Shame on him, he thought.

"Here she comes," Olivia said softly.

Scott looked from his sister to Dylan. "I heard you. Both of you," he said, rising to his feet as Meg approached the table.

He held out her chair so she could sit, and Emilio returned with their food. The rest of the meal passed with general conversation. Scott was ready to get Meg home and fix things between them as best he could. The rest would come with time. He hoped.

*　　*　　*

Meg walked out of the restaurant and headed for the parking garage. The balmy air settled on her shoulders, too humid for comfort. She glanced at Scott, who seemed … calmer somehow. Which she didn't understand considering how intense so much of the conversation had been.

"Would it be okay if we stopped by my apartment on the way home?" she asked. They weren't too far from her place, so it wasn't out of the way. "I need more comfortable clothes, since I'm not going to be working, and while I'm there, I can grab my mail."

"Not a problem."

He braced his hand on the small of her back as they walked, and she did her best not to visibly react to his warm touch. Even if her body responded to him, would always respond to him, her brain was sending out warning signals to keep her emotional distance.

"I should have told you what I knew about the Ashtons," he said, surprising her. "I just figured you needed time to breathe before we jumped into that again on Wednesday."

She smiled grimly. "And you didn't know Luke was going to tell me first, which pissed you off."

"It's not that," he said, too quickly.

She deliberately cleared her throat, giving him a chance to change his mind.

"Okay, it's that," he said, obviously caught. "It's just... I wanted to be the one to tell you."

They paused outside the garage where they'd parked. "But you didn't. You decided to wait. We've talked about this already. You can't keep making decisions about what I need to know and when."

"You're right." He tilted his head, looking into her eyes as he spoke.

"I am?"

"But you have to admit we've had a lot of different emotional topics going on. I can't always know what's best or get it right."

She sighed, and the weight on her shoulders eased a little. "I'll give you that." Nothing between them was simple. Or easy. Not anymore.

His hand slid from her back to her hip, and he turned her to face him. "Don't give up on me," he said in a thick tone, his eyes a darker navy than she could remember seeing them, his expression serious. "I know I've given you reason not to trust me. I came on strong, and I pulled back … but that's over now."

She shook her head, not understanding. But her heart beat faster inside her chest.

"You've been great," she told him honestly. "You stepped up when nobody else did. You're making sure both me and my baby are safe. I'm grateful."

His hand tightened on her waist. "I don't want your gratitude, baby."

Her heart tripped at his use of the word in *that* tone. He sounded more like the Scott who'd pushed his way into her life and promised he'd never leave and less like the man who'd pulled away emotionally.

She ran her tongue over her lips, gratified when his eyes followed the movement. "What do you want?"

"You," he said gruffly, pulling her against him and kissing her hard.

If he was trying to make a point, he did it well, his tongue swiping over her lips, demanding entry she willingly gave. As he consumed her mouth, he held her hard against his hips, her body well aware of his hard length pressing into her. Excitement and yearning filled her veins, a liquid pulsing desire that spoke of true need and longing for this man. She kissed him back with everything she had, ignoring the warnings that tried to intrude.

Suddenly a loud car horn sounded, and she jumped back. "Get a room!" a man yelled out the window of a car that had pulled up the ramp of the parking garage. She and Scott were blocking the driver from leaving.

Certain she was blushing, she stepped to the side and waved. "Sorry," she called toward the car's open window as Scott joined her, laughing.

They didn't discuss the moment outside the garage or the words he'd spoken, and Meg was grateful. Her head was spinning as it was, and she needed time to unwind and just *be*, something Scott seemed to sense.

Once they arrived at her apartment, they stopped at the mailboxes downstairs, and she pulled out the stack of letters and a bulky soft package that barely fit into the box.

Scott waited while she packed up a few more casual tops and other things she'd forgotten before rejoining him. "I'm just going to look through the mail here, so I only take what I need. I have my checkbook so I can mail out any bills I don't do online."

"Take your time."

She sorted junk mail from bills, tossing the former into the trash. Her eye caught on the package, and she picked it up, looking for a return address. "Huh."

"What is it?" Scott asked.

"I don't know." She grabbed a scissor from a drawer in the kitchen and cut straight across the top. She turned it upside down and shrieked as a small baby doll, the head separated from the body, fell onto the table.

Meg stared, unable to believe what she was seeing.

"Holy shit," Scott muttered. "Don't touch it." He grabbed her and pulled her back, away from the doll.

Shaking, Meg glanced up at him. "He's lost his mind," she whispered.

"He's not going to get near you or the baby," he promised, wrapping his arm around her and leading her away from the counter and the offending package.

"Let me just call someone to come pick this up and dust for prints. I don't expect to turn up anything, but maybe we'll get lucky."

Meg didn't reply. She couldn't. She was too nauseous and scared to even try. This time, a friend of Scott's from the force arrived, not a cop he didn't know. The man took more interest in Meg and her case, and they processed the doll for evidence, but like Scott, he didn't hold out much hope for prints.

Through it all, Scott held her hand or wrapped her in his protective embrace, and she didn't think it made her weak to accept his comfort. Mike wanted to kill her baby. No way would she let it happen. Neither, she believed, would Scott, and that was the only thing that kept her marginally sane.

A very long while later, they returned to Scott's house. She still didn't speak, and he didn't push, which she appreciated. His steady presence was all she needed.

He locked up the house and set the alarm before joining her in the bedroom. She'd already washed up, changed into a nightie, and climbed into bed. Scott slid in beside her, pulling her tight against his hard body, holding her until she fell into a fitful sleep.

*   *   *

The beginning of the week passed slowly, the damned baby doll never far from her thoughts. Scott offered to stay home with her, but she insisted he go to work and get used to his new job and let the guys see him pulling his weight as boss. He needed to do that for himself and for Tyler, and Meg didn't want to grow to rely on him any more than she already did. The house was alarmed, Rick sat outside, and Meg was as safe as possible. For now.

By the time Wednesday arrived, Meg was edgy from a combination of boredom and angry frustration. Mike had made her a prisoner in Scott's house, unable to live her life, and she resented him for that. The Ashtons had invited Meg to meet at their Palm Beach country club. She explained she was bringing Scott as her friend and as her bodyguard because she wanted them to understand just how serious a threat their son posed to her and her baby. She pressed her hand against her growing belly protectively, nervous now that she had to leave the safety of the house.

She dressed in a pair of knit leggings and matching top, a gray and white outfit that was true maternity wear. It seemed as if her small belly had popped overnight, her baby making its presence well and truly known. A flutter of excitement filled her along with a healthy dose of trepidation. The thought of a baby was way different than the reality, and now she'd get a feel for how Scott would react when he noticed her body's changes.

He'd asked her not to give up on him, and she'd felt the intensity and seriousness in his tone and his actions. Ever since Sunday night, he'd been back to the Scott who'd barreled his way into her life and made her the center of his world. She just didn't know if it would last, and she didn't need the added emotional stress.

Scott drove them north to Palm Beach, where the Ashtons lived, and the long ride passed in tense silence. The tension wasn't between her and Scott, however; it was Meg's nerves that had completely overtaken her. It didn't help when they pulled up to the front of the club, an imposing structure with white pillars and lush palm trees surrounding the building. She felt way out of her league.

Valets were waiting to take their car. Scott accepted the ticket before walking around the car, toward her. He always took her breath away, and today was no different. He'd showered and shaved, so not only did he look good, he smelled delicious, his musky scent calling to her body and arousing her despite the time and place.

He'd dressed up in a pair of black slacks and a pale blue long-sleeve button-down dress shirt. Blue was clearly his favorite color, and it had quickly become hers because of how the color set off his gorgeous eyes. He also wore a black sport jacket, his holstered gun hidden at his side. Though she hated the idea of the weapon, she felt so much better knowing he was with her and armed. She didn't want to think the older couple would set her up by bringing Mike, but anything was possible. Mike was tracking her or following her somehow, and today's meeting wouldn't go unnoticed. Her stomach flipped painfully at the thought.

"Are you okay? You didn't say a word on the drive up," Scott said, his big hand cupping her elbow as he joined her.

"No," she said honestly. "But I have to do this." She pulled in a deep breath of air.

"Well, you're not alone." He pressed his forehead to hers, the gesture both tender and intimate, and her entire body flooded with warmth and heat.

"I know." She pulled back and managed a smile to reassure him. "Let's get this over with."

He studied her face, as if making sure she really was ready, before nodding. "Okay."

A little while later, introductions complete, they were seated at a small round table, facing the older couple. Lydia seemed nervous, which ironically put Meg more at ease.

"Thank you for meeting with us," Walter said. He had gray hair and, now that she allowed herself to really look at him, kind eyes.

Meg swallowed hard. "You're welcome."

Lydia leaned forward in her seat. "How are you

feeling?" she asked Meg.

"I'm fine. I was pretty lucky early on. The morning sickness wasn't that bad, and now I'm feeling good."

The older woman nodded. "That's good." She paused before speaking. "I wanted so badly to carry a child." She smiled, but her eyes appeared sad. "It wasn't meant to be for us, but we were lucky enough to be able to adopt."

Meg didn't know what to say, so she remained silent. Beside her but beneath the table, Scott reached over and clasped her hand in his. He always knew when to offer silent support, as if he could read her mind or her moods.

"I've always been hands-on with children's charities, and it made sense to me to adopt a baby that not everyone else would want." Lydia wrapped her heavily jeweled fingers around a cup of hot tea, as if needing the warmth. "Mike had fetal alcohol effects," she explained. "We didn't know what the impact would be on him long term, but we thought we were equipped to handle it."

As if sensing she needed his strength, Walter reached over and took his wife's hand away from the cup, covering it with his own. Meg watched them, surprised. She hadn't expected a loving couple, and both her heart and her mind told her this wasn't a performance for her sake. The affection between them was real.

"I take it Mike was ... more than you anticipated?" Meg asked gently.

Lydia's eyes filled with tears and she nodded. "He didn't have the physical problems sometimes associated with a mother who drinks, but he had the behavioral issues. As time went on, things got worse. And with the inherited addictive tendencies, when he started drinking at a young age and hanging out with the wrong kids..." She shook her head. "We tried counseling, out treatment, in treatment..." She trailed off, her voice catching.

"I had no idea," Meg said. "When I met Mike, I didn't notice anything wrong. He was working construction. I met his friends... There were no warning signs. Until he lost his job, and then he changed."

She recalled that night, the first display of temper, and she shuddered. He hadn't hit her then. In fact, he'd never laid a hand on her until she'd told him about the baby, but the sudden shift in his mood had been terrifying.

"Losing a job is something that happens often, I'm sorry to say," Walter said.

"He did get another one quickly, so I didn't think much of it. Except he was laid off pretty fast from there too." Meg took a sip of water. "He used to say you wouldn't help him because he wouldn't be the person you wanted him to be, that your expectations were too high. Then again, he found my expectations too high, and all I wanted him to do was pay his share of the rent and come home at night instead of partying with his friends."

Scott stiffened beside her, clearly not happy with her replaying of her past.

"It's not your fault," Walter said. "My son is good at manipulative behavior and getting what he wants from people." He met his wife's gaze with a sad nod.

"This is all well and good, but we need to figure out how to get Mike to back off and leave Meg alone. He's threatened to *help* her get rid of the baby, and he just sent a beheaded doll as a warning in the mail," Scott said, his angry tone reflecting his frustration.

"Oh my. I'm so sorry." Lydia shook her head, unable to meet Meg's gaze. "What can we do?"

"From what Mike has said, this is all about money. Just assure him that if he signs the papers relinquishing his rights to the baby, you won't cut him off. That will take the edge off his anger and get him to back off and leave Meg alone."

Meg knew it wasn't a guarantee, but she agreed with Scott it might be a start.

"I'm sorry but we can't," Walter said.

Chapter Eleven

"Can't? Or won't?" Scott asked the older man, disappointed for Meg's sake that the last twenty minutes of understanding and kindness had still led to disappointment.

"Scott—" Meg said in warning.

"No, he's entitled to his opinion. We've heard it all before," Walter said.

"Have you ever dealt with an addict?" Lydia asked.

Meg shook her head.

"Well, it's simple. We can't enable Mike in order to ensure good behavior. It doesn't work, it won't last, and in the end, more trouble will come down the road. You're asking me to keep paying him, which will only feed his addiction. And I promise you, it won't keep you safe," Walter explained, and in that moment, he appeared older than he had on first meeting. When speaking of his son's problems, the lines in his face, the extreme sadness, were more pronounced.

"Meg, it's not that we don't want to help, it's that we've had almost thirty years of experience raising him, the last I don't know how many years being taught how to deal with addictive behavior," Lydia said, her imploring stare on Meg's as she spoke.

"Then what do you suggest?" Scott asked, well and truly pissed off.

"Unfortunately, I don't have a suggestion, and I know that's not what you want to hear." Walter met Scott's gaze. "If you need money to help keep the mother of my grandchild safe, just say the word—"

"Thanks but I've got this," he said too harshly.

Meg squeezed his leg beneath the table. Scott took the hint, but he didn't need it. He wanted to be offended by the offer ... but he wasn't. He also wanted to dislike these people because of who their son was ... and couldn't. He wouldn't want to be judged by his father. He couldn't do the same to this couple.

"Meg, I meant what I said when I came to see you at school. I'd like to be part of the baby's life. But I'd like to get to know you too. We have time before the baby is born. You can get to know me ... us," Lydia said. "You can decide for yourself once you know us more."

Scott felt Meg's shock in the stiffness of her body. "I'd like that," she said softly.

He understood. She had nobody in the way of family. Not like he did. These people were offering her and, by extension, her child a bond she was lacking. Scott wanted that for her. Just like he wanted her to think of his mother and siblings as her family too. But first he had to get her to accept him as a permanent part of her life.

With the difficult discussions behind them, they ate and talked about neutral subjects. They asked Meg about her childhood, where she'd gone to college, and learned more about her in general. He watched as she slowly opened up to them, something he knew from personal experience she didn't do easily.

By the time the meal ended, Meg had relaxed, and Scott had a better handle on the Ashtons. He could honestly say he was comfortable with Meg spending time in their company, not that she needed his permission, he thought wryly.

They walked out the front entrance into the warm sunshine. Scott glanced around, seeing only two valets in green jackets and a taxicab idling not far from where the men would bring his truck.

"Thank you so much for coming. It was a pleasure getting to know you," Lydia said to Meg, pulling her into an embrace.

Meg hugged the woman, patting her back awkwardly, but in her expression, Scott could see the hope of acceptance, of family. It was everything Scott wanted for her, and he, too, prayed the couple lived up to the promise.

Walter stepped closer, grasping Meg's hand in his. "You're a lovely young woman."

She blushed, that pink flush Scott liked seeing on her cheeks. "Thank you."

"Traitors!"

The shouted word startled everyone.

Scott spun as a man strode forward from the yellow taxi. Meg turned fast, her expression turning to one of horror. "Mike," she whispered at the same moment Scott recognized him.

The man wore dirty clothes, his hair hadn't been washed in too long, and his eyes were bloodshot from drugs or alcohol.

"Mike?" Lydia gasped, her face turning pale.

And Walter, who still held Meg's hand, stared in shock at his son—who had a small revolver in his hand.

Scott reached for and raised his gun without thinking twice, training the weapon on Mike Ashton.

"How could you choose that bitch over me?" Mike asked, the hand holding the gun shaking uncontrollably.

"Calm down, son," Walter said, dropping Meg's hand and holding his up in the air. "You're my child.

Nothing changes that," he said, speaking slowly and calmly.

"Except that baby." Eyes wild, Mike swung the gun toward Meg and lunged forward, shooting as he moved.

On instinct, Scott fired at Mike, diving for Meg at the same time. Walter was closer and threw Meg to the ground, but his shocked scream told Scott he'd taken the bullet meant for Meg.

"Call 911," Scott shouted to one of the valets who had ducked behind the small desk where he worked. "And keep everyone else away!"

Scott immediately spun toward Meg, calling her name.

"Fine," she called out.

Scott began breathing again, everything around them happening at warp speed.

Crying, Lydia rolled her husband off of Meg while Scott kept his gun trained on Mike, who lay groaning on the ground. Blood spread through the man's shirt, but it looked like the original injury was in the upper right shoulder, a result of Scott's preoccupation with getting Meg out of harm's way.

Mike flinched, moving his good arm, and Scott kicked the man's gun farther away, in case the asshole thought he had a chance of getting to the weapon.

"Come on, honey. Talk to me," Lydia said to her

husband.

"I'm okay." Walter spoke in a weak voice. "Just my damn arm."

Scott let out a relieved breath that Walter's injury wasn't life threatening. From the corner of his eye, Scott saw Meg rise to her feet, while at the same time, the sound of sirens cut into the silence.

Without warning, Meg barreled into him, wrapping her arms around him tight. "Oh my God, I was so scared."

Her voice sounded muffled in his shirt, her tears dampening the fabric, and his heart clenched inside his chest. The same heart he'd thought closed up for good only a short month ago.

"Join the club, baby. If this bastard had shot you and I was a few feet away and didn't stop him…" He couldn't finish the thought, nausea filling him at the notion. "How's Walter?"

"Hurting, but I think he's okay."

Two police cars and an ambulance screeched to a halt. The men in blue surrounded Scott, and he placed both weapons on the ground, kicking them toward the police. Though it took awhile, with Scott no longer being in possession of a badge, the police eventually sorted out the facts.

Mike had been hit in the upper shoulder, and the paramedics quickly stabilized him, then loaded him into the ambulance for the trip to the hospital. With a police escort. He'd soon be read his rights and booked.

Another set of paramedics worked on Walter.

Lydia stepped back to give them room. She headed straight for Scott, her face streaked with tears.

Scott drew a breath before facing the woman whose son he had shot. "Mrs. Ashton…"

"Walter and I just had to say thank you."

"What?" Scott asked, confused.

The older woman stepped forward and hugged Scott tight, taking him completely off guard. "You didn't kill my son. Thank you."

"Mrs. Ashton!" a paramedic called out. "We need to go."

She eased back. "You two take care. I'll be in touch."

"Bye," Meg whispered.

"Good luck," Scott said to her retreating back before turning to Meg. Makeup smudged beneath her eyes, tears stained her cheeks, but her brown eyes sparkled with life, and that was all Scott cared about.

"She's right. You didn't kill him."

"Don't give me so much credit." He hated to burst her bubble or perception of him, but it couldn't be helped. "In the split second I had, I aimed dead center, but I was trying to get to you at the same time, and the shot went wide."

She sucked in a surprised gasp. "Well, then things work out the way they're supposed to. I'd hate for you to have Mike's death on your conscience. And I wouldn't want it on mine either."

It wouldn't have been either of their faults, but he wasn't going to argue with her. He brushed her hair off her face and tipped her chin up. "I said I'd keep you safe, and that was too damned close for comfort."

She nodded. "He can't walk away from this, right? It's attempted murder, right? He's going to jail?"

"He sure as hell is."

She closed her eyes and sighed. "Thank God. It's over."

It sure as hell was, Scott thought, pulling her close, breathing in the fragrant scent of her hair. Mike's reign of terror was over. And so was Meg's need to remain with Scott. In his house, in his arms, and in his life.

*   *   *

In a daze, Meg walked into Scott's house. She headed straight for the master bathroom and began stripping off her clothes piece by piece, shedding the memories along with the shirt that was covered in Walter Ashton's blood. He'd thrown himself over her, putting himself in front of a bullet to save Meg's life from a shot *Mike* had fired.

Mike, who she'd cared for, if not loved. Mike who'd fathered her child. With shaking hands, she turned on the water, hoping the heat of the shower would warm the chill that spread through her from inside and out. She stuck her hand into the spray, testing the temperature before stepping inside.

"You didn't waste a second," Scott said, joining her in the bathroom.

She glanced at him through the see-through enclosure, watching his eyes heat as he took in her naked body.

"I had to get out of those clothes." Her voice cracked, and she turned away, stepping under the hot spray to wash away her tears before he could see.

The sound of the shower door opening and closing drew her attention, and then Scott was there. He pulled her into his arms and held her tight as she cried, letting out all the pent-up emotion of the last few weeks and the hell Mike had caused. She hadn't really let herself fall apart, and now that the adrenaline rush ebbed, she sobbed without holding back.

When she'd finally cried herself out, she became aware of Scott's body, his hard muscles, hair-roughened skin, and the gentle yet protective way he held her close. One hand stroked her hair, the other wrapped around her waist as he waited for her to pull herself together.

Once she was ready, she drew a deep breath and glanced up at him. "Thank you. I needed that."

His smile didn't reach his eyes. "I hope that's the last time you cry over that bastard ever again."

She managed a nod. "Me too." She tipped her head up and tried to clean up her face, knowing her makeup had to be dripping down her cheeks.

"Here. Let me." Scott pulled a washcloth from a towel bar and wiped beneath her eyes, gently cleaning her up.

She didn't have the strength to be embarrassed and let him do what he wanted.

"There. All set," he said.

She gave him a shaky smile. "Thank you."

"My *pleasure*." His low voice and tone had an entirely different meaning, and her body perked up, suddenly awake and aware of him as a man. A very sexy man she desired with every fiber of her being.

Without speaking, he reached over and picked up a bar of soap, then proceeded to lather up his hands before kneeling at her feet. He placed the bar of soap on the floor beside him and cupped her ankle in his big hands.

She glanced down at his dark hair, his sexy pose, and her nipples peaked with desire, her breasts suddenly heavy, her pussy throbbing with need.

"What are you doing?" she asked thickly.

He glanced up, his eyes as dark as she'd ever seen them. "Taking care of you," he said, then bent to his task.

He soaped her skin, starting at her feet and moving upward, massaging her muscles with tender care. First he pressed his thumbs into her calves, slicked his hands up behind her knees—an erogenous zone she hadn't known she possessed—before graduating to her thighs. His talented fingers reached higher quickly, and she sucked in a breath as he slid his thumbs along the crease between her thigh and her slick outer folds.

She grasped on to his shoulders and held on, fingers digging into his skin as he soaped around her sex, fingers easing over her nearly bare mound but never touching where she needed him most. She arched her hips forward. He chuckled, low and deep, pausing only to soap up his hands again and keep moving, up her belly, over her breasts, paying special attention there but not stopping in his quest to clean her completely.

It was as if he understood how fragile today had made her feel, how out of control and afraid, and he was here to help her rinse off all traces of the horrific experience.

He slicked his hands over her shoulders, down her arms, threading their fingers together almost symbolically, his heavy-lidded, aroused gaze meeting hers. That's when it dawned on her.

Scott wasn't speaking. There was no dirty talk. No sexy descriptions of what he was going to do to her. No teasing comments about how many times he planned to make her come. Instead, there was an intensity and seriousness to his touch and his expression she'd never seen before.

It was as if he were memorizing every second, every bit of her because now that the danger had passed, this was their last time together. And though she knew it to be true, the pain of that thought lanced through her heart.

There was so much unspoken in the steamy bathroom and between them, but she couldn't bring herself to think beyond the here and now. All she wanted was to feel, and Scott was so capable of making her do that. He unhooked the handheld shower sprayer and rinsed her off, gliding his fingers over the soap, pushing the foam off her skin, helping the soft sprinkling of water do its job.

Once she was clean, he knelt before her once more. Her sex clenched in anticipation, but his next move was so much different than she expected. So much … more.

He braced his hands on her hips and leaned close, pressing his lips to her now slightly visible belly. Her throat swelled, her heart filled, and intense feelings of longing swept through her, rendering her unable to think, let alone speak. He glanced up long enough to meet her gaze, to hold on, to force her to look into his eyes, which were glittering with the same raw emotion pulsing through her.

He rose and slammed his hand against the faucet, shutting off the water, then opened the shower door and guided her to the floor mat. He wrapped her in a towel and gently patted her dry, keeping her wrapped and warm. He grabbed another towel and dried himself. He dropped his towel to the floor and tugged hers off, too, before sweeping her into his arms.

She wrapped her arms around his neck and held on, nuzzling her cheek against his, breathing in the warm, clean scent of his skin. She never thought she'd have even this much with any man, and Scott Dare exceeded all her dreams and expectations.

Even now, as he carried her determinedly into the bedroom and placed her in the center of his large bed, he was her white knight. She withheld her smile at the thought, knowing he wouldn't like it.

Coming over her, he bracketed her between his thighs, pinning her pelvis to the mattress with his naked body as he stared into her eyes.

"You've been quiet," she said, needing to break the silence, to know what was going on in his head even if she didn't want to hear.

"I'm not sure you want to know," he said, his jaw tight.

She had a hard time looking past his bronzed, muscular chest that was just begging for her touch.

"Probably not," she agreed. "But we're going to have to deal with it sooner or later." Not that she could concentrate at all with his hard, hot sex throbbing against hers.

"Yes, we are." He lifted his hips and slid his cock over her damp sex.

She closed her eyes, and sparks flickered behind her lids at the erotic feel of him gliding against her. She whimpered and bent her knees, wanting him to take her hard and deep.

"No, Meg. Look at me."

She forced herself to meet his determined gaze. "I know you don't want to rely on me. That you need to stand on your own, and I respect that." He leaned over and touched his forehead to hers before looking into her eyes once more. "I respect *you*."

She swallowed hard, waiting for his next words.

"And know this," he continued. "I'll always give you what you need even if it's not what I want."

"What do *you* want?" she asked.

He shook his head, his lips lifting slightly. "I can't believe you have to ask. I want you, Meg. I *love you*."

The words echoed inside her head, as if she were

hearing them for the very first time ever. And in a way, she was. Nobody who'd said them to her in the past had meant them. Not the way Scott so clearly did. She'd never known her father, and she couldn't remember ever hearing those three words from her mother. And come on, *let me move in, Meg. You know I love you,* wasn't the same as this heartfelt declaration.

She'd never forget hearing Scott say it now, and her eyes filled with tears. "I love you too."

"Thank God." Scott felt the sheen of perspiration on his forehead and lower back. Sheer nerves. He'd never been so scared as when he'd taken that leap, waiting to hear if she felt the same way. He might not get to keep her now, but he wouldn't lose her forever. He had to believe that or he'd lose what was left of his mind.

He had more to say. So much more, but now wasn't the time. "I need to be inside you," he told her instead.

She smiled, laughing through tears. "That's my sweet-talking man."

Yeah, he was hers. Even if she moved out and insisted on doing things on her own, he'd be there until she came around. But that was talk for *after.*

He braced his hands on either side of her shoulders, flexed his hips, and drove home. Home being the only word crashing through his mind as he sheathed himself completely inside her warm, wet heat. He groaned as she cushioned him in her silken walls.

"Fuck," he muttered. "You feel so good." Beneath him, Meg arched her back, pulling him deeper when he hadn't thought it possible.

"I need to feel you everywhere," she said, her fingernails scraping against his scalp.

He groaned and began to move, thrusting in and out, totally in tune to her every sigh, moan, and shift of her body. And though his orgasm was building fast, it was obvious so was hers, her breathing coming more rapidly, the tugs on his hair more urgent.

She wrapped her legs around his waist, locking him against her body, taking what she needed from him as they drove each other toward an explosive climax. Heat and fire sizzled up his spine, his balls drawing up tight, the need to come warring with the desire to wait for her to tip over first.

"Oh God, Scott, love you," she cried out at the moment she peaked and fell, her slick walls clasping him tight and sending him spiraling out of control as he came.

"Oh fuck, Meg, love you," he said, his hips slamming into hers, his hot come filling her. *Love you*, he thought. *Don't leave me*, came next. But with everything in him, he knew that she would.

Awhile later, they lay in his big bed, the silence

surrounding them almost painful. Meg curled into his side, one hand on his chest, her naked body pressing against his. He savored the warmth and the feel of her wrapped up in him.

"I have to leave," she said softly, her tears dripping onto his bare chest.

The words hurt as much if not more than he'd expected. "Yeah, I know. But I have to tell you a few things before you do."

She sniffed and nodded.

His throat hurt, but he forced out the words. "If you're leaving because at any point I convinced you that I don't want a family or the fucking fairy tale I said doesn't exist, that's just not true anymore."

She stiffened, and he used her shock to his advantage, pulling himself over her, staring into her beautiful face.

"Dare I ask what changed your mind?" she asked.

The answer was easy. "You did. I can't live without you, and I don't want to. I love you. I am going to love that baby, and I want us to be a family." The words, once out, felt freeing. "I mean that. I don't want you to leave. I want you to stay here, with me. But if you don't stay, make sure it's for the right reasons."

"Scott—"

He silenced her with a long kiss, losing himself in her sweetness before pulling back. "Go because you need to prove to yourself that you can get by without a man. Without me. But know that I'll be here waiting when you're ready to fight for us."

She cupped his face and ran her hands over his clean-shaven cheeks. "I love you too. And you're saying everything I ever wanted to hear."

"But you're leaving." He braced himself for the final slam.

In her big brown eyes, Scott saw all the hurt and pain he himself was feeling.

She nodded. "Like you said, I have to prove to myself I can be an adult and not the needy woman who chose a man, any man, as long as she wasn't alone."

He was so damned surprised she didn't know herself yet. Didn't see herself the way he did, as a strong, self-sufficient, woman capable of raising a baby alone. But she didn't have to.

"Okay," he said, forcing himself to roll to the side, off of her lush body. He felt the chill deep in his bones. "I'm not going to stop you or beg you to stay."

She bit down on her trembling lower lip, her eyes still damp. "You're not?"

He shook his head, his clenched fists the only outward sign of how difficult this was for him. But inside he was dying. "I told you, I'll always give you what you need. So if you need to go, go."

Scott didn't have a plan. He didn't know what he'd do or how he'd get her back. Instead, he breathed in deeply, searching for a sense of calm he didn't feel, only to inhale the musky scent of sex and Meg.

*   *   *

Meg drove herself home and Scott didn't argue. She didn't know whether to laugh or cry at the fact that she totally missed him telling her what he wanted her to do. It wasn't that she'd always listen, more that his expectations told her he was thinking about her, her welfare, and that he cared. Like he cared enough to let her pack up her things and move out.

Idiot, a very large part of her brain told her. Who leaves a man who loves her with everything he has? Who walks away from the best thing that ever happened to her? Apparently, she realized, as she strode into the apartment she called home, the empty apartment that no longer felt like home, Meg wasn't finished making stupid, wrong, bad-for-her decisions.

Because as she unpacked her clothes and toiletries, she couldn't help but feel like she was in a strange place. A place she'd lived both with Mike and alone. And as she picked up the phone to order pizza, because she had no food in her pantry or refrigerator, she was forced to ask herself, was being alone taking a stand? Who was she proving a point to? Not herself.

She was miserable. She had a lump in her throat, her chest hurt, and she missed Scott like crazy. What was she accomplishing?

She sat alone at her kitchen table, a box of uneaten pizza in front of her, and she hated herself for her decision.

Her phone rang, and she dove for it on the first ring like a crazy person, but it wasn't Scott, it was Lydia Ashton.

"Hi, Lydia. How's Walter?" Meg asked. She'd called the hospital, but since she wasn't family, they wouldn't give her any information.

"He's doing well, thank you. In fact, they're releasing him as long as he promises to take it easy, and you can bet I'll make sure that he does," the other woman said, relief in her voice.

"I ... I don't know how to thank him for what he did for me," Meg said.

"Don't worry, honey. He knows."

Meg sighed.

"There's something else I wanted to tell you. It's about Mike."

Meg stiffened but forced herself to remain calm and listen. "Yes?"

"Walter and I talked to Mike. We told him we would pay for his lawyer if he signed away his rights to the baby."

"What?" Meg asked startled.

"We explained that if he did, we'd hire a lawyer whose goal was to get him into a prison with treatment for addiction. If he doesn't sign the papers, he can go with a public defender and hope for the best," Lydia said, her voice cracking with emotion.

It was hard not to feel sorry for her as the mother of a man with serious issues. "Do you think he'll sign?" Meg asked.

"I do. He swore he would because the thought of being left high and dry by us is more than he can handle. He realizes there is no situation that will give him access to money he can use to fuel his addiction. That should also help."

"Lydia, thank you," Meg said again. "I don't know what more to say." The couple had chosen their grandchild over their son, and Meg would be forever grateful. "I'd like to come visit when Walter is up to it."

"We'd love that," Lydia said. "We are looking forward to getting to know you."

Meg smiled. "I feel the same way."

"Good. And make sure that nice Scott Dare drives you. It's a long ride. You need to take care of yourself," Lydia reminded her.

A knot of emotion welled inside Meg at the sincere sound of caring in the woman's voice. She couldn't bring herself to explain why Scott wouldn't be with her or that she'd brought that on herself.

"Take care and we'll talk soon," Lydia said.

"Good-bye." Meg disconnected the call and placed her phone onto the kitchen table.

A glance told her there were no missed calls or texts while she'd been on the phone. Why would there be? Scott had offered Meg everything she'd ever wanted. He told her he'd always give her what she wanted. And she'd basically informed him she wanted to be alone.

Brilliant, Meg.

She headed for the kitchen and grabbed foil, wrapping the individual slices up and placing them in the freezer for another time. No way could she eat them now.

She turned to go into her bedroom and paused. Was she really going to do this? Continue on with a decision she'd made that, in her heart and soul, she knew was wrong for her?

Or was she going to correct it?

* * *

Scott appreciated his siblings more than anyone, but he really didn't want company. Unfortunately, Olivia had heard from Tyler about what had happened this morning with Mike. Olivia had called Scott, asking to speak to Meg. Which meant he'd had to tell his sister that Meg had gone home. And that had led to her arriving on his doorstep with Avery to check on him. Luckily for him, Olivia had left Dylan at home. Not so luckily, his sisters were in the mood to talk, at least, Olivia was.

"Give it time. Meg's been through a huge trauma. She needs to settle, you know?" Olivia propped her feet on a large ottoman in front of her chair in the family room.

"Meg made it clear what she wanted from day one. I just barreled forward, thinking I knew better," Scott muttered. And he'd had his heart gutted in the process.

Not that he was giving up. He'd just retreated in order to regroup. And though he hated to give his bossy sister credit for anything, she was right. He had to give Meg the space she needed.

He glanced over at Avery, who stared out the window beside her chair in pensive silence. He cocked his gaze her way and met Olivia's gaze.

She shrugged her shoulders, meaning she didn't know what was going on with her either.

"Listen, I appreciate you guys coming over, but I'm fine." Or he would be once they left and he could drown his sorrows in Jack. "I'm sure Dylan would rather have you home."

Olivia eyed him warily. "Are you sure?"

"Definitely." He rose from his seat.

"Come on, Avery. I'll drop you off on my way home," Olivia said.

Scott strode over to his youngest sister and grasped both her shoulders. "I want my bubbly sister back. If that means I have to kick some guitarist ass, I have no problem doing it."

Avery glanced up at him, an appreciative smile on her face. "It's a lot of things, all of which I'm dealing with. I promise. No need to get all big brother on Grey. Especially since he's a client."

Scott blinked in surprise. "You know that Lola Corbin hired us to handle the band's security?"

Avery grinned. "I know a lot of things that would surprise you," she said and patted his cheek. "Don't worry about me. Just figure out a way to get Meg back. I want you to be happy."

Scott's heart melted at that. He pulled her into a tight hug. "I won't let anyone hurt you, baby girl."

Avery squeezed him back. "And I love you for it."

He walked his sisters through the front hall. "Thanks for coming by, and drive safe," he said as he opened the door ... and came face-to-face with the last person he expected to see.

"Meg!" Olivia exclaimed. "I'm so glad you're okay."

"Thank you." Meg glanced nervously at Scott as she replied.

"Hi, Meg. I'm glad you're out of danger too," Avery said.

"And we were just leaving," Olivia said, grasping Avery's hand and pulling her out the door.

God bless his sister for having the good sense to get out quickly, Scott thought, turning his attention to the woman at his doorstep.

"Hey," he said, his grateful gaze raking over her. Though he'd seen her a few hours ago, she looked more tired than he remembered, and he wanted to pull her into his arms and carry her off to bed.

Then he remembered he didn't have that right anymore.

"Did you forget something?" he asked, wondering why else she'd be here, even as he drank her in.

Her long legs peeked out beneath a tank top dress. No makeup on her pretty face. And those big brown eyes stared into his.

"Nope. I didn't forget anything."

"Then you're here because…?" he asked, tamping down on that elusive thing called hope.

"I came home."

He blinked, stunned. "You're…"

"Home. If you still want me, I mean." She bit into her lower lip. "I walked into my apartment, and I knew immediately I'd made a huge mistake. I was so wrapped up in thinking I had to stand on my own, I walked away from everything I wanted. Everything that was good and right in my life. And that's you. So I came back."

His heart started beating again. Damned if he'd realized it had stopped, but now that Meg was here, back... "For how long?" he asked.

"Forever if you'll have me. I want everything you said. You, me, this baby. I want to be a family, and I want *you*." She stepped forward, and he was there, pulling her into his arms and sealing his lips hard on hers.

Relief poured through Meg as he kissed her thoroughly, as if he'd never let her go. The entire drive over, she'd been afraid he'd changed his mind, that she'd pushed him to his limit, that he'd turn her away.

She threaded her fingers through his hair and kissed him back with everything she had. When they broke for air, she met his inky gaze. "I'm sorry."

He shook his head. "Don't apologize for what you needed, baby. You're here now, and we both know it's because you thought things through and you want to be."

"I do. I really do."

The sexy grin edging his lips was one she could look at all day and never get enough. "Okay, then, but know this."

"Hmm?"

"I'm not letting you go. Ever." He lifted her into his arms, and she held on tight as he walked into the house and slammed the door closed behind them.

Carly Phillips

Stay tuned for more DARE family stories in 2015 and beyond!

Thank you so much for reading *Dare to Hold*. I would appreciate it if you would help others enjoy this book too. Please recommend to others and leave a review. More Dare to Love series stories coming in 2015 and beyond! Read on for an excerpt for the next book, DARE TO ROCK, Avery Dare and Grey Kingston's story and for information on keeping up with Carly and the next Dare to Love series books!

Dare to Love Series

Book 1: Dare to Love (Ian & Riley)

Book 2: Dare to Desire (Alex & Madison)

Book 3: Dare to Surrender (Gabe & Isabelle)

Book 4: Dare to Submit (Decklan & Amanda)

Book 5: Dare to Touch (Olivia & Dylan)

Book 6: Dare to Hold (Scott & Meg)

Book 7: Dare to Rock (Avery & Grey) 8/4/15

Book 8: Dare to Seduce (Lucy & Max) coming soon

each book can stand alone for your reading enjoyment

**The Dare to Love series is ongoing. Each Dare sibling will get a story!

**Each book stands alone but also reads best if order for maximum reading enjoyment.

*Dare to Surrender and Dare to Submit are about the

NY Dare cousins: These exceptionally hotter type books while at heart still being a Carly Phillips story.

Keep up with Carly and her upcoming books:

Website:
www.carlyphillips.com

Sign up for Carly's Newsletter:
www.carlyphillips.com/newsletter-sign-up

Carly on Facebook:
www.facebook.com/CarlyPhillipsFanPage

Carly on Twitter:
www.twitter.com/carlyphillips

CARLY'S MONTHLY CONTEST!

Visit: www.carlyphillips.com/newsletter-sign-up and enter for a chance to win a $25 gift card! You'll also automatically be added to her newsletter list so you can keep up on the newest releases!

And now an excerpt from *Dare to Rock* ...

Coming 8/4/15 and available for preorder!

Dare to Rock
Excerpt

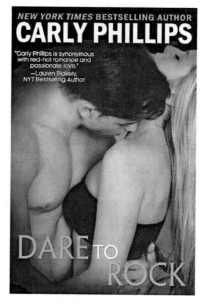

Preorder DARE TO ROCK

DARE TO ROCK

Avery Dare & Grey Kingston
Dare to Love Series #7

NY Times Bestselling Author Carly Phillips turns up the heat in her newest sexy contemporary romance series, and introduces you to the Dare family... siblings shaped by a father's secrets and betrayal.

Avery Dare lives a quiet life in Miami as an online fashion/makeup video blogger. She has good friends, a close, large family and if her love life is lacking, she likes it that way. But when she receives an invitation to one of her ex's concerts along with an invitation to meet him back stage, she decides to take the risk ... and comes face to face with the reality of his rock star lifestyle – the press, the crowds, and the half naked groupies.

At eighteen, Grey Kingston left everything he knew and loved behind to seek fame and fortune as a rock star, and he found it as the lead guitarist and singer for the band, Tangled Royal. Fans adore him, women throw themselves at him, and he can afford everything he couldn't growing up. Yet at the height of his career, he's ready to walk away and return home to a simpler life ... and the woman he left behind.

Except moving on isn't as easy as Grey would like. When Avery is threatened by a stalker, it becomes evident Grey's fans not only don't want him to retire, they don't want Avery in his life either. And Avery isn't sure she wants the pressures that are part of Grey's life ... but she doesn't want to lose him again, either. Can their recently renewed love survive the fallout?

Prologue

S weat poured off Grey Kingston's body and his heart beat a too rapid rhythm, the high and adrenaline rush from his performance still pulsing through his veins as he walked into the lounge backstage. He pulled off his soaked shirt and tossed it onto the floor, grateful for the stocked room and waiting pile of towels. He grabbed one and wiped his face and hair dry, deliberately trying to slow his breathing.

The sound of Tangled Royal fans stomping their feet and demanding an encore echoed through the walls, but the band had performed their final set. But his pulse still soared as he glanced at the door.

"Did she pick up the ticket?" Grey asked Simon Colson, their manager, who was busy texting on his phone.

"What? Who?" Simon shoved his phone into his back pocket. "Great concert by the way," he said to

Grey, and the rest of the band.

Lola Corbin, their lead singer and Grey's best friend, was still bouncing in her heels, not yet coming down from their shared high either. "We did rock it," she said, tossing her dark hair over her shoulder.

Milo Davis, their bassist, grunted something and fell into a chair in the corner. Grey narrowed his gaze. Milo barely had the energy for a full concert these days and that worried him.

But right now Grey had bigger concerns and turned to Simon. "I asked you if Avery Dare picked up the VIP tickets I told you to leave at the box office."

"Dunno."

Grey scowled at his manager's I don't give a shit tone. More and more lately, Simon's lack of consideration about what the band wanted grated on Grey's nerves. Lola might be considering using him for her solo career but anything Grey did going forward wouldn't be with the man.

At least he'd left the tickets. He'd be out of a job if he screwed with Grey on this. "Fucking find out."

"What's so special about this piece of ass?" Simon barely got the words out because Grey grabbed him by his collared shirt and pinned him up against the wall.

"Talk about her like that again and you're done."

"Whoah." Lola put her petite body between them, pushing Grey away from their manager. "Everyone breathe," she muttered. "You. Go take a walk and calm down before your company shows up," she ordered Grey.

He stormed off, missing whatever lecture she gave to Simon next.

Though the man had done his job well, helping maneuver Tangled Royal to the top, he cared about the bottom line and not much else. Especially not the fact that Tangled Royal was more than a band, people with real feelings, issues and lives. No wonder Simon didn't believe how serious both Grey and Lola were about changing their futures.

Danny Bills, their drummer, already had a wife and two daughters who lived in L.A. He was ready for home time and everyone knew it. Milo was another story. If he didn't stop the drugs he wouldn't have a future.

As for Grey, he hoped for more than the travel and fame that had been so important to him way back when.

His eyes flickered to the door. No sign of Avery. He tipped his head back, wondering if she'd come back stage or ignore the invitation ... and him. His stomach gripped painfully at the thought of not seeing her again. She was the one person who not only understood the loner musician he'd been as a teen, but who grounded him when he threatened to spiral.

Along with her soft voice, that thick mane of dark hair, and those lavender like eyes, she'd burrowed someplace deep inside him.

But she hadn't been enough to hold him, not when fame, fortune and the need to be something *more*, lived within him. But it was Avery whose face he saw in the nameless women he'd fucked over the years. Avery whose belief in him kept him going when times were hard. Funny how that worked. He wondered if she thought of him over the years and if she was as hyped up about possibly seeing him again now.

A loud scream brought him out of his thoughts. He glanced up as a group of women poured into the room. Half dressed, teased hair, too much makeup and enough perfume to make him gag. Fucking Simon never listened. He'd specifically told Simon not to let any of their crazed female fans backstage.

Grey pushed himself off the wall and stormed over to his manager. "I told you no more groupies after concerts." Especially not tonight when he was expecting Avery.

He shot a disgusted look at the women fawning over a dazed Milo. They wouldn't give a shit if he was dead, they'd want a piece of him anyway. The thought disgusted him.

"Wasn't me, security obviously didn't get the message," Simon said.

"Grey!"

He glanced up just as a woman he recognized threw herself at him, wrapping her arms around his neck. Her big, fake breasts pressed uncomfortably against his chest, and she raked her clawed nails through his scalp.

"Baby you were so good! So hot. I just knew you were singing directly to me."

He choked over her sickly sweet scent. More because he'd been dumb enough to screw her once, years ago, after a concert and way too much to drink. She'd been trailing after him ever since. He attempted to detangle himself from her, but she wasn't letting go. *This* was why it was time to call it quits.

"Marco!" Grey called out for the bodyguard who usually prevented him from being mauled, but the guy was nowhere to be found. Beside him, Simon merely grinned, pleased with the fact that the band was liked, wanted and making him money.

"Back off," Grey said to the woman, pulling at her arms but she had them locked tight around him.

"Baby, you don't mean that."

"Oh I really fucking do." He glanced over hoping to catch Lola or Danny's attention and get help when his gaze fell on the woman who had just entered the room.

She was so beautiful she took his breath away.

Wholesome yet sexy, creamy skin, gorgeous silky hair and a nervous expression on her face as she looked around, a stark contrast to the harsher looking groupies who followed the band.

And she hadn't seen him yet.

Left with no choice, he was going to have to physically extricate himself from the clinging octopus of a woman even if he hurt her. He grasped her around the waist, intending to shove hard, just as Avery's gaze landed on him, her eyes flickering from him to the woman he *looked* like he was holding in his arms.

A flash of emotion flickered across her expressive face. Everything from awareness, shock, disgust and hurt all showed before she swung around and headed for the door.

"Avery!" He called her name loud enough to be heard across the room, while shoving the groupie, sending her tripping backward.

She wailed and began crying, and her friends surrounded her but Grey ignored her in favor of Avery.

He reached the door just as she paused and turned to him. "I shouldn't have come."

"Yes, you should have." She was so close he could see the light sprinkling of freckles on the bridge of her nose and his heart threatened to pound out of his chest. "This isn't what it looks like."

She tipped her head to one side. "But it *is* your life.

The one you worked hard to achieve and … I'm happy for you." But the words were at odds with the sad smile lifting her glossed lips. "It's good to see you, Grey." She raised a hand his way before she turned and walked out.

Shit. "Avery!" He stepped into the hall.

"Grey! I've got Rolling Stone on the phone and they want an interview. I need an answer now," Simon said, seeking his attention.

A glanced back told Grey that Avery had gotten lost in the crowd held back by security. His head pounding, he walked back inside, ignoring his manager.

"Was that her?" Lola came up beside him, her voice soothing in light of the chaos swirling around him.

"Was is the right word," he muttered. "I can't do this anymore, Lo."

"I hear you. It's not good for us. Rep doesn't like the crap that comes with our kind of life either," she said of her serious boyfriend who was the Miami Thunder's hugely successful wide receiver. "I want to be around during the season and he worries when we're on the road and he can't be there." She rested her head on his arm. "We do have a tour to finish though."

"We do," he agreed. "But afterwards? I'm coming home." And he was going to get his girl.

Carly Phillips

Chapter One

Three Months Later

A very Dare stared at the blank screen on her computer, surprised that no snappy topic or product came to mind for an upcoming blog, despite the piles of free product that had been sent to her for testing. One of the perks of being a professional blogger with a huge online social media presence, she received packages from companies looking for her to pimp their goods. It was a cool job she'd somehow turned into a career and she loved it. She enjoyed interacting with people online, discussing things they had in common, helping people be their better self, as she liked to call it.

She'd always managed to keep her online persona and her real self separate. Even if her sister and friends read and interacted there, her readers looked at Avery as one of them ... someone who loved the newest

Louis Vuitton handbag but wouldn't necessarily be able to go out and afford to buy it. She wasn't about flaunting her family name or wealth and apparently her fans enjoyed that about her too.

A familiar *ding* alerted her to incoming emails and she clicked back to her mail program. An alert from a local gossip blog caught her eye and she read the subject.

Reports of Tangled Royal breakup confirmed.

Avery's stomach lurched at the mention of the band's name and she bit down on her lower lip, memories of going to visit her high school boyfriend after his concert weighing on her. It wasn't like she was naïve or stupid. She knew what kind of life a rock star of Grey's magnitude lived. And if she hadn't known, she'd been forced to see the pictures and snippets of information over the years by virtue of the same magazines she read to keep her blog current.

But seeing pictures of a guy she'd known in the past and having to face it up close and personal when she'd thought she would be seeing him in private … that had hurt. And the vision of the bleached blonde wrapped around his body while other women, dressed equally as skanky, surrounded the band, merely reminded Avery of how different their lifestyles were. And how they each, always, wanted very different things. So she'd left the room before they could do more than look into each other's eyes … knowing she had to protect herself because one look at his handsome face, more mature, but still the same features she used to love, had hit her hard.

He hadn't given up. Over the last few weeks, every time she posted something meaningful on her blog, like a hot new handbag she liked or a perfume she sampled, the same product ended up being sent to her doorstep. Giftwrapped beautifully, with a short card attached. *I'm sorry – G. Give me another chance – G. Call you when I'm back in town – G. Can't wait to see you – G. Missed you all these years – G.*

Yeah, that last one got to her most. Because she'd missed him too. Then, as routinely as they'd arrived, the gifts had stopped. And she couldn't help but wonder if he'd decided she wasn't worth the effort, not when he had all those groupies at his disposal. She'd tried to put him out of her mind, but it wasn't easy.

Her finger hovered over the keyboard before she finally gave in and opened the email and read the alert in its entirety.

*Grey Kingston **sighted in and around Miami and South Beach** over the last week while bassist Milo Davis settles into L.A., adding fuel to the rumors that the band is going their separate ways.*

So he was here. Back in Miami. And so much for his promise to contact her when he was back in town. She shouldn't be all that surprised. Just another let down by the man who'd stolen her heart. Only recently had she come to realize she'd never really gotten it back.

"You okay?" her roommate asked, peeking into her bedroom.

Avery pushed her chair back and grinned at Ella Williams, her once pen pal and best friend for what felt like forever. Ella had moved into the spare bedroom when Avery's sister, Olivia, moved out and married Dylan Rhodes.

"I am awesome," Avery said, turning her back on the screen behind her.

"And I don't believe you." Ella plopped down on Avery's bed, curling her legs beneath her. Her damp, light brown hair hung around her face and because she had silky fine hair, she wouldn't have to do much to make it shine. Unlike Avery who had to work hard to get the flat-ironed look.

"You're awesome?" Ella asked, in a mimic of Avery's forced high pitched tone. She pinned Avery with a knowing stare and didn't look away.

"Okay fine. I'm not awesome." She'd never been able to lie to Ella, not since the day they'd met in the hospital when they were nine years old, each donating bone marrow to a relative.

"I'm guessing Grey Kingston has something to do with you being distracted?" Ella asked.

Avery pursed her lips and nodded. Though she hadn't told her family what happened when she'd gone to see Grey backstage, she had confided in Ella. It wasn't that she didn't want to tell Olivia, but the time had never been right. First, Dylan's old friend Meg had been in the hospital and they'd been busy with her troubles, and after Olivia's life had fallen into place with a man she loved and a new start. Avery hadn't wanted to burden her sister with her own issues.

"Still no word from him?" Ella asked.

"No. And I shouldn't care. I mean I'm the one who told him to stop texting me and to focus on his tour."

"But he didn't listen, if those gifts were anything to go by."

"No. He said he'd be in touch the next time he was in Miami." Avery picked at a nonexistent piece of lint on her silk pants.

"I'm sensing there's more?" Ella pushed. Ella always pushed, never allowing Avery to escape into herself as she was prone to do.

She swallowed over the surprisingly painful lump in her throat. "I just read he's been back in town for the last week or so."

"And he still hasn't been in touch."

"No. And I shouldn't care! I don't want to care."

"But you do." Ella patted the space beside her and Avery crawled onto the mattress and curled up against her pillows.

"I'm being ridiculous. I should be relieved. I saw him with those women and I ran from everything his lifestyle represents didn't I?"

"You did."

"So why do I care that he decided I'm not worth it?"

"That's not what he decided!" Ella exclaimed, shaking her head in frustration. "If I could wrap my hands around your father's neck for all the insecurities he caused you, I would."

Avery blinked back tears, surprised by the heavy emotion in her friend's voice.

"I've known you for a long time and you've told me things your siblings don't even know, right?"

Avery nodded. Ella had always been her safe place. Grey had too ... once. She pushed the thought aside.

"Then you know I'm right. You still feel like all you were worth to your dad was the bone marrow to save a sister you didn't even know about. Then Grey left you to find fame and fortune and you've convinced yourself nobody views you as worthy enough. Well I'm here to tell you that you are." She grasped

Avery's hands. "Mr. Tangled Royal would be lucky to have you in his life. Not the other way around."

Avery blew out a deep breath. "You're right. Dealing with him has made me feel like I'm back in high school all over again and I'm not. I've moved on."

Ella eyed her with a mixture of amusement and laughter. "Now I don't know if I'd go that far."

Avery smacked her with the nearest throw pillow and her friend laughed.

"But I would say you've grown up a lot since you two saw each other last. With a little luck, so has he. So if he does get in touch and he wants to get together, I think you owe it to yourself to meet up with him. Think closure, if nothing else."

"When did you get so smart?" Avery asked.

"The day you became my best friend." Ella grinned. "Besides it's easy to give advice to someone else about their love life."

As open as Ella was with most things, she didn't talk much about her own guy situation. Mainly because she claimed there wasn't anything to discuss, which made no sense because Ella was pretty, sweet, and any time she dressed up, she outshined everyone around her. She deserved a great man in her life.

"Anything you want to talk about?" Avery asked, hoping for once her friend would open up.

"Nope. I actually have to get to work. I promised

my boss I'd meet with a new photographer she's considering hiring." Ella was an assistant to an up and coming fashion designer based out of Miami. Another reason they were such good friends, they shared a love of clothes, makeup and design.

"Okay, well thanks for the talk," Avery said.

"Any time." Ella pushed herself off the bed just as Avery's cell dinged from across the room, announcing a text.

"Toss me that before you go?"

Ella grabbed the phone from beside the computer and squealed as she handed Avery the cell. "Looks like Mr. Tangled Royal surfaced."

Avery's eyes opened wide as she stared at Grey's name on the screen.

"I'm calling later for all the details," Ella called out with glee, before heading out of the room.

*   *   *

Grey listened to the cell phone ring, wondering if Avery would answer or if he'd waited too long. Tangled Royal had finished up their tour, throughout which Grey had sent a steady stream of gifts corresponding to the things Avery said she liked on her blog, *Avery's Attitude*. He wished he could take credit for being so creatively smart, but it had been Lola's idea, as a way to get back into Avery's good graces. Or at the very least, it was a start.

The first gift and card he'd sent contained his private cell and he'd asked her to text him. She had. Which had started a stilted and hesitant back and forth between them. Lola was right, it had been a good opening gambit. Then Milo had OD'd and everything in his life had screeched to a halt as they'd tried to help their friend. The early days of rehab hadn't been easy. He'd threatened to leave, Lola had cried, Grey had begged and done everything short of taking his best friend's place himself, to get him to stick it out.

By then the band had fulfilled their concert commitments. Lola had cemented her relationship with Rep and decided to buy a place on secluded, private Star Island, and Grey had put in motion the process of buying out both Lola and Rep's leases. The condo board had finally approved his application, speeding things up because of his interest in the two apartments on the same floor. Lola's side, he intended to turn into a sound proof studio.

He was finally ready to come home.

All of which had occupied his time. Not to the exclusion of Avery. Never that. He just wanted to be settled before approaching her again. If they had any chance of seeing what could be in the future, she had to believe the life he desired now wasn't the one he'd wanted then. Or the one she'd seen backstage.

Just as he thought her voicemail would pick up, he

heard her familiar voice. "Hello?"

The soft, dulcet tones settled something deep in his bones. "Hey there," he said, suddenly at a loss for how to handle her.

"This is a surprise."

"I told you I'd call when I got to town." And she hadn't believed him. The thought showed him just how much work he had ahead of him. Good thing he wasn't afraid of working for what he wanted.

She cleared her throat. "So you just got back?"

"No, I've been here for a week or so. I wanted …" Fuck. How did he say this? "I'd rather fill you in in person."

"Grey, I'm really not sure –"

"Give me a chance to just talk to you. If after that you don't even want to be friends, I'll back off." He was lying through his teeth but that was okay. All he wanted, needed, was the opportunity to test their chemistry again. To let her see that what they'd shared as kids could be even more solid as adults.

The silence on the other end of the phone nearly killed him. But he waited, opting not to pressure her.

"Okay," she finally agreed. "But someplace out of the way. Quiet."

"I already made a reservation at Quinto's," he said of a mom and pop Mexican place they'd frequented as kids. "Saturday night if you're free."

"I loved that restaurant. And I haven't been there

in years." She blew out a long breath he heard over the line. "Pretty sure of yourself," she finally muttered.

"Pretty hopeful," he corrected her. "Can you make it?"

She hesitated before answering. "Yes."

He refrained from pumping his fist in the air.

"What time?" she asked.

"How is eight?"

"That works. I'll meet you there."

"No. I'll pick you up at seven thirty."

"Grey —"

"Avery —" He repeated back, like he used to every time she'd tried to argue with him.

Her light laughter eased the heavy weight on his chest.

"Fine. I already know you don't need my address." Her tone softened at the unspoken reminder of the many gifts he'd sent over.

"No, I don't. I'll see you at seven thirty on Saturday. And Avery?"

"Hmm?"

"I can't wait to see you," he said, hanging up before she could answer … or worse, not say the same.

Carly Phillips

Preorder DARE TO ROCK

About the Author

N.Y. Times and *USA Today* Bestselling Author Carly Phillips has written over 40 sexy contemporary romance novels. After a successful 15 year career with various New York publishing houses, Carly made the leap to Indie author, with the goal of giving her readers more books at a faster pace at a better price. Carly lives in Purchase, NY with her family, two nearly adult daughters and two crazy dogs who star on her Facebook Fan Page and website. She's a writer, a knitter of sorts, a wife, and a mom. In addition, she's a Twitter and Internet junkie and is always around to interact with her readers.

CARLY'S BOOKLIST
by Series

Below are links to my series on my website
where you will find buy links for each novel!

Dare to Love Series

carlyphillips.com/category/books/?series=dare-to-love

Dare to Love

Dare to Desire

Dare to Surrender

Dare to Submit

Dare to Touch

Dare to Hold

Dare to Rock

Dare to Seduce

Carly Classics

carlyphillips.com/category/books/?series=carly-classics-books

The Right Choice

Suddenly Love (formerly titled Kismet)

Perfect Partners

Unexpected Chances (formerly titled Midnight Angel)

Carly's Earlier Traditionally Published Books

Serendipity Series

carlyphillips.com/category/books/?series=serendipity-series

Serendipity

Destiny

Karma

Serendipity's Finest Series

carlyphillips.com/category/books/?series=serendipitys-finest

Perfect Fit

Perfect Fling

Perfect Together

Serendipity Novellas

carlyphillips.com/category/books/?series=serendipity-novellas

Fated

Hot Summer Nights (Perfect Stranger)

Bachelor Blog Series

carlyphillips.com/category/books/?series=bachelor-blog-series

Kiss Me If You Can

Love Me If You Dare

Lucky Series

carlyphillips.com/category/books/?series=lucky-series

Lucky Charm

Lucky Streak

Lucky Break

Ty and Hunter Series
carlyphillips.com/category/books/?series=ty-hunter-series

Cross My Heart

Sealed with a Kiss

Hot Zone Series
carlyphillips.com/category/books/?series=hot-zone-series

Hot Stuff

Hot Number

Hot Item

Hot Property

Costas Sisters Series
carlyphillips.com/category/books/?series=costas-sisters-series

Summer Lovin'

Under the Boardwalk

Chandler Brothers Series
carlyphillips.com/category/books/?series=chandler-brothers-series

The Bachelor

The Playboy

The Heartbreaker

Stand Alone Titles
carlyphillips.com/category/books/?series=other-books

Brazen

Seduce Me

Secret Fantasy

CPSIA information can be obtained at www.ICGtesting.com
Printed in the USA
LVOW12s0402060515

437406LV00016B/124/P